S0-ACO-159

"Tristan?" she whispered. "You're real."

It wasn't a question. Not exactly. Because he was real. She knew it. The water dripping off his hair and clothes was wet on her skin. The face she was touching was sickly white, yes, but it was warm and fleshy and, most important, it was not fading before her eyes. She grabbed a handful of hair and squeezed it. Her hand came away soaking wet. She looked at it and laughed, but the laugh turned into a sob.

His brown eyes turned darker. "I'm real," he said, his mouth stretching into a wry smile as a dampness glistened in his eyes.

She sobbed again and put her hand over her mouth, hoping to stop them before they stole what little oxygen she had left in her lungs.

"It's okay, San. It's okay."

"Okay? Is it?" she snapped, still stunned by the vision before her. "Where did you come from? We. Buried. You."

SECURITY BREACH

MALLORY KANE

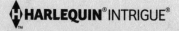
HARLEQUIN® INTRIGUE®

If you purchased this book without a cover you should be aware
that this book is stolen property. It was reported as "unsold and
destroyed" to the publisher, and neither the author nor the
publisher has received any payment for this "stripped book."

This one is for the readers. Thank you for liking my books.
Thanks for the letters and emails and Facebook posts. For your
insights, your compliments and your critiques. I love you all.

ISBN-13: 978-0-373-69841-7

Security Breach

Copyright © 2015 by Rickey R. Mallory

Recycling programs
for this product may
not exist in your area.

All rights reserved. Except for use in any review, the reproduction or
utilization of this work in whole or in part in any form by any electronic,
mechanical or other means, now known or hereinafter invented, including
xerography, photocopying and recording, or in any information storage
or retrieval system, is forbidden without the written permission of the
publisher, Harlequin Enterprises Limited, 225 Duncan Mill Road,
Don Mills, Ontario M3B 3K9, Canada.

This is a work of fiction. Names, characters, places and incidents are
either the product of the author's imagination or are used fictitiously,
and any resemblance to actual persons, living or dead, business
establishments, events or locales is entirely coincidental.

This edition published by arrangement with Harlequin Books S.A.

For questions and comments about the quality of this book,
please contact us at CustomerService@Harlequin.com.

® and TM are trademarks of Harlequin Enterprises Limited or its
corporate affiliates. Trademarks indicated with ® are registered in the
United States Patent and Trademark Office, the Canadian Intellectual
Property Office and in other countries.

Printed in U.S.A.

Mallory Kane has two great reasons for loving to write. Her mother, a librarian, taught her to love and respect books. Her father could hold listeners spellbound for hours with his stories. His oral histories are chronicled in numerous places, including the Library of Congress Veterans History Project. He was always her biggest fan. To learn more about Mallory, visit her online at mallorykane.com.

Books by Mallory Kane

HARLEQUIN INTRIGUE

Bayou Bonne Chance series

Under Suspicion
Security Breach

The Delancey Dynasty series

Double-Edged Detective
The Pediatrician's Personal Protector
Private Security
Death of a Beauty Queen
Star Witness
Special Forces Father
Dirty Little Secrets
Sanctuary in Chef Voleur
Blood Ties in Chef Voleur

Black Hills Brotherhood series

His Best Friend's Baby
The Sharpshooter's Secret Son
The Colonel's Widow

Visit the Author Profile page at Harlequin.com for more titles.

CAST OF CHARACTERS

Tristan DuChaud—The Homeland Security agent and soon-to-be father didn't die on an oil rig in the Gulf of Mexico, but he's badly injured. When he finds out his wife is back in Bayou Bonne Chance, he knows there is something in the house that could put her in danger. Then he sneaks in to grab the item and leave and she catches him. Now not only must he continue his battle to stop terrorists from smuggling automatic handguns into the US, but he must also face the one person he could never fool.

Sandy DuChaud—The lovely pregnant widow is stunned when she finds out her husband is still alive, and angry that he did not contact her. But as she realizes how badly he's injured and how desperate he is to keep her and their child safe as well as stop the terrorists trying to destroy the US from the inside, she begins to see that he's not the man he was. He's better.

Boudreau—A born-and-bred Cajun, Boudreau has lived in the swamp since anyone can remember and has always watched over Tristan DuChaud. He finds and rescues Tristan and cares for him like a father for his son. He stays by Tristan's side, although he disapproves of the chances his young friend is taking. He would give his life for Tristan, and as the danger escalates and their odds for survival go down, he just might have to.

Murray Cho—The Vietnamese fisherman, who moved away from Bonne Chance after the violence in his old seafood warehouse where smuggled weapons were stored, is spying on Sandy DuChaud. When caught by Boudreau, Cho reluctantly reveals that his son has been kidnapped and will be killed if Cho doesn't find proof that Tristan DuChaud is still alive. Is Cho telling the truth or is he working with the man behind the terrorist plot to draw Tristan out into the open?

Vernon Lee—Vernon Lee is a multibillionaire who owned the oil rig where Tristan DuChaud was purportedly killed and where the smuggling operation was based. He seeks proof as to whether Tristan DuChaud is alive or dead. The Homeland Security agent holds evidence that could implicate Lee in the terrorist smuggling operation and in Tristan's attempted murder. As soon as his men catch DuChaud and his Cajun friend, Lee plans to have them all killed. He doesn't like loose ends.

Chapter One

Murray Cho had always worked hard, as a boy in Vietnam after his parents were killed and in America after he immigrated. But the so-called land of opportunity was not accurately named, at least not for a poor immigrant from Vietnam. Eventually, he managed to buy a shrimp boat in a small town in South Louisiana on Bayou Bonne Chance and make enough of a living to take a wife and have a son.

But when Patrick was five, Murray's wife ran off, leaving him to rear his son alone. He and Patrick had made it just fine until two months ago, when gun smugglers hid their booty in Murray's shrimp warehouse and hurt his reputation. So Murray moved himself, Patrick and his shrimp boat to a dock near Gulfport.

For a couple of weeks, Murray had thought the move was a good one, until an ominous voice on his phone had shattered his peaceful fisherman's existence. The voice threatened harm to his son, Patrick, if he didn't follow their directions with no questions.

It wasn't difficult to figure out why the men had chosen him. He was at once familiar and suspicious to the people of Bonne Chance. Brandishing a gun at and threatening the smugglers who'd used the old seafood warehouse he'd bought as a depository for the automatic handguns they were smuggling into the United States had not helped his reputation in the town.

Stealing a laptop from Tristan DuChaud's home had been a piece of cake, once Patrick had shown him how to disarm a security system. He didn't want to know how his son knew that. All he wanted to do was leave the laptop computer where he'd been instructed and go back to his simple life. With any luck that was the last he'd hear from the men.

Murray reattached the rope he'd just mended to the rear of the boat, and then headed across the dock and through the gate, locking it behind him. The RV that he and Patrick lived in was across the parking lot. It was tiny but it served. He slept in the bedroom and the boy slept on the couch.

Murray opened the door quietly, frowning to find it unlocked. Patrick always promised to lock the door before he went to sleep, but he was barely eighteen. He had trouble remembering to close the door, much less lock it.

The interior of the RV was dark and quiet. It was after ten o'clock on a school night. His son should be home studying or in bed. Irritated and a little worried, Murray dialed Patrick's number. No answer. Then before the display went off, the phone rang.

"Patrick, where are you?" he snapped.

"Murray Cho?" a familiar voice said. It was the same man who'd sent him into Tristan's house for the laptop.

Murray's heart pounded. "Where's Patrick? If you've done something to him—"

"Listen to me," the voice said. "We've got your son. He's alive—for now."

"What? For now? What's going on? I want to speak to him."

"I said *listen*! You did a good job of getting the laptop. Now we've got another job for you. DuChaud's wife is back in the DuChaud house, by herself. My boss is wondering why she didn't stay with her mother-in-law. What do you know about Tristan DuChaud?"

The dread that had squeezed his chest the first time the man had called him seized him again. "DuChaud?" Murray stammered. "He's dead."

"Is he?" the voice on the phone asked. "How do you know?"

"Th-there was a funeral," Murray stammered. "Please. Let me talk to Patrick."

"We'll make you a deal. You get us proof that DuChaud is alive and we won't kill your son."

Murray's heart seized in terror at the man's words. "No! Please! I'll do anything, but don't hurt my son."

The man sighed. "Come on, Cho. You think begging me is going to do any good? I've got orders from my boss to get this information or my ass is on the line. I picked you because you're known around that area and nobody would think it unusual if you were seen around the dock or the DuChaud house."

"I—I don't understand," Murray stammered.

"Look, we're not bad people. We don't want to hurt you or your kid, but if we don't get this job done it's going to hurt us—permanently. That's another reason I picked you. Because you have a kid, you're motivated. So get me some proof. If he's alive, my boss wants to see proof. If he's dead—" The man gave a little snort. "That'll be harder to prove."

"Who's your boss?"

"Nope. Now, Cho, you should know I can't tell you that. Just do what you're told and don't ask questions."

Murray shook his head numbly. He had no choice. His son's life was on the line.

"We'll take care of your son as long as we can. You need to concentrate on what I'm saying."

Murray did his best to remember what the man had said the boss wanted. "Y-your boss wants proof Tristan DuChaud is alive? But he's dead. They buried his body. I can't prove he's alive."

"You're not helping yourself or your boy by arguing. We're going to check with you every day and find out what you're doing. This better not take long, Cho. And if you even think about going to the authorities, your son will suffer, and I do mean suffer." The phone went dead. The caller had hung up.

Murray stared at the phone's screen until it went black while the man's voice echoed in his ears. *You get us proof...and we won't kill your son.*

He had to do something. Had to rescue Patrick. But how? How could he prove that a dead man was alive?

It was at dusk, the end of the day, when she missed Tristan the most. A thousand years ago, someone in Britain had known enough about loneliness to name this time of day the gloaming. A little later, it was called eventide. These days, most people said twilight or dusk. Pretty words, but depressing, according to Sandy DuChaud.

Sandy preferred the sunrise. The beginning of the day. Each rising sun was a new promise, a bright beginning that called to her. She'd loved to roust Tristan out of bed, thrust a hot mug of coffee into his hand and make him watch the sunrise with her. And he in turn had delighted in making her take a walk with him at sunset. With Tristan at her side, she'd begun to get over her innate sadness at the fading of the sun's light.

But Tristan was gone now, and even the sunrise didn't cheer her.

"Do you know what today is, bean?" Sandy asked her unborn baby as she rubbed the sore spot on her baby bump where he liked to kick. "No? Little bean, you need to keep up. It's been two months since your daddy died—" Her voice gave out and her breath caught in a sob.

"Come on," she said. "We need to unpack." Yesterday afternoon, she'd walked into their house on the outskirts of Bonne Chance, Louisiana, for the first time since the day after her husband's funeral. It had been so quiet, so empty, so lonely.

At first, she had been overwhelmed with grief and sadness that Tristan wasn't there and would never be there again. But as she'd stood looking out the French doors past the patio and the driveway to the graceful, drooping trees, vines and Spanish moss of Bayou Bonne Chance, she'd felt a serenity inside her like nothing she'd ever felt before.

The faint sound of the surf and the mellow ring of the wind chimes on the patio washed over her, adding to her peace and calm.

This was why she'd come back to Bonne Chance and their home and all the memories, good and bad. She could hear Tristan's laughter in the organic, spiritual sounds of nature. It called to her as the sun always had.

Forgetting about unpacking, she slid open the French doors and walked outside. The air in June seldom got cool in South Louisiana. Oh, sometimes a storm would send a chilly breeze in from the Gulf. But anyone who lived in the Deep South knew that chilly and cool were not the same thing.

Cool was pleasant—afternoons on the front porch with the ceiling fan rotating, watermelon or iced tea and desultory conversation about nothing more important than how well the fish were biting. Chilly, on the other hand, was a damp breeze that cut through any material, even wool, and made fingers and toes stiff and cold.

"We seem to be all about word choices today, bean," she said. Lifting her head, she let the evening breeze blow her hair back from her face. When she opened her eyes, there was still a faint pink glow in the western sky.

"Okay. Yes. The sunset is kind of pretty," she admitted reluctantly. "I'll give you that. But it will be completely dark in less than fifteen minutes. I'd planned to walk over to the dock and back this afternoon, but I let the time get away from me. It's too close to dark now."

She'd walked over there late the day before. She still wasn't sure why. Maybe hoping to feel Tristan's presence there, where he'd spent so much time. That dock had been his second favorite place all through his childhood. Boudreau's cabin had been his first.

Tristan had always liked swimming in the Gulf this time of the day. He'd pointed out to her that as the sun went down, everything calmed. The breezes that normally seemed to carry sound died, the birds and animals quieted, and the waters of the Gulf became calm and slick as glass. He'd said it was as if the whole world hushed in respect for vespers.

Sandy recalled the dark form she'd seen in the water, diving and swimming out beyond the shallows at the dock. She'd been looking into the setting sun and so all she could see was a sinuous silhouette sliding between the waves. She'd thought it was a dolphin.

But now, thinking back, she could convince herself it looked human.

The sky was getting darker every second. As Sandy turned back toward the house, a faint whispering stopped her. It sounded like voices.

She went still, listening. Disturbed by her sudden anxiety, the baby kicked. Sandy patted her belly reassuringly.

Within a few seconds, the sounds became repetitive and she realized her ears had played tricks on her. The susurrus noise wasn't voices. It was leaves and twigs rustling as something or someone moved through the tangled jungle of the swamp. Something or someone large.

But who—or what? And was it as close as it sounded?

She shivered. There were a lot of wild animals in the swamp, some very large, like alligators or bears. But she'd lived here all her life. It wasn't the prospect of meeting a wild animal that made her tremble.

It was the memory of the dark form swimming gracefully in the Gulf. Had it been a person? Who would be swimming at dusk and then walking through the swamp, the way Tristan once had?

No. She had to stop imagining that each breeze that lifted the curtains or each murmur of waves licking the shore could be Tristan—or his ghost.

There had been nothing ghostly about whatever was moving through the tangle of trees and vines just now. Those sounds were real.

There was no reason she could think of for anyone to be on DuChaud property, not at this time of day— or any time of day, actually. The DuChaud's home was eight miles from the town of Bonne Chance. Everybody knew where the beautiful hand-built house was, but the road from town turned from asphalt to shells and gravel about two miles away and ended at the DuChaud's patio. It was not a road that invited casual drivers.

A different noise broke the silence of the early darkness, again faint, but recognizable. The sound of snapping twigs and crunching leaves.

Whatever or whoever was out there was on the move and didn't care who heard him. Sandy inched her way backward, away from the trees and toward her house, both hands cradling her tummy protectively. She ran through the French doors as if the hounds of hell were nipping at her heels, locked them and set the alarm.

Only then did she breathe a sigh of relief. "Sorry, bean," she muttered. "I know it's silly, but I think I scared myself."

All at once, her eyes began stinging. Blinking furiously, she tried to make the tears disappear, but they still welled and slipped down her cheeks.

"Damn it, I don't want to be afraid in my house. But like it or not, you and I are here alone. We have to be careful. Besides, that's our dock—your daddy's dock," she said, her voice tightening with grief.

"Oh, Tristan," she whispered. "I need you so much. I'm doing my best to live without you. Why are you still. Right. Here?" She slapped her forehead with two stiff fingers.

"Right here in the very front of my brain. Why aren't you fading, like a perfect memory should—" Her voice cracked and a couple of sobs escaped her throat. She pressed her lips together, hoping to hold in any more sobs. She didn't want to cry. The more upset she got, the more restless the little bean.

In all the years she'd been married to Tristan, in all the years she'd known him before that—essentially their whole lives—she'd never been afraid of anything. But the sound of footsteps had spooked her.

"Don't worry, bean. I'm not turning into a scaredy-cat. I came back here for the peace and quiet, and no alligator or poacher—or whatever that was—is going to scare me away." Her brave words made her feel better, and as she relaxed, she realized how tired she was.

Yawning, she checked the alarm system and armed the doors and windows, then headed toward the master bedroom.

As she passed the closed door to her office, which they'd converted into a nursery, she realized she hadn't even thought about checking her email. Too distracted by memories, she supposed.

When she turned on the light, the desktop was empty. Her laptop wasn't there, where it always sat. Automatically, she glanced around as if it might have gotten set aside by someone during the time she'd been in Baton Rouge with her mother-in-law.

But by whom? And when? A chill ran down her spine at the thought of someone coming into her house.

No, she told herself. *Don't start panicking. Think rationally about who of all the people who must have had access to the house could have done it.* Obviously Maddy Tierney or Zach Winter, but Maddy would have told her, right? So…people from the crime scene unit? But all the evidence of Maddy's kidnapping by the captain of the *Pleiades Seagull* was in the master bedroom. Why would they need to take her laptop computer?

But if not them? Then she had a thought that sent her heart hammering. What if it had been Tristan? What if he was out there, hiding, and needed something from the laptop.

"Stop it!" she cried. "You can't go there every time something odd happens or you hear a strange sound. He's dead and nothing is going to bring him back to life!" Blinking, she forced away all her silly romantic thoughts of Tristan out there somewhere, alive and hurt.

Forget all the evidence about how he had died. Forget everything except one fact. He'd gone overboard into the dark, dangerous water and had never come out. That, if nothing else, told her he was really dead. If he were still alive, he would move heaven and earth to get to her. Tristan would die before he'd allow her to believe he was dead.

With a quick shake of her head, she forced away thoughts of Tristan and concentrated on the missing laptop.

Before she jumped to any conclusions, she should check with Maddy and Zach. They may have had to confiscate it so the hard drive and memory cards could be reviewed.

Maybe Homeland Security or the NSA had needed it for evidence. That made sense, except for the fact that there was nothing on her laptop that could possibly be interesting to anyone other than herself.

She checked her watch. It was just after ten. That was eleven Eastern time. She hesitated for a second, then pulled out her phone. Maddy had told her to call anytime if she needed anything.

When her friend answered, she blurted out, "Maddy, did you or Zach take my laptop?"

"What? Sandy? Are you all right?"

"I'm fine. Did either of you take my computer, or see someone else take it?"

"It's not there?"

"No. It always sits on my desk in the nursery. Always. And it's not there."

"No, we didn't. We searched it. Remember, you gave us the password. We went through all the saved files, looking for anything that might have been related to Tristan's death or the smuggling, but it was there when I left." Maddy paused for a beat. "Have you seen any other signs that someone has been in your house?"

Sandy's tummy did a flip, which woke up the baby. He wriggled and kicked. "I don't think so. The nursery is the only room I hadn't been in. You're sure it was here when you guys left?"

"I am," Maddy said. "Did you check with the crime scene unit or the sheriff?"

"No," Sandy said. "I called you first."

"Well, you need to call them. If they took it you should have gotten a receipt, but people forget things."

"So it disappeared after you left." She paused, thinking. "Wait. Come to think of it, the alarm wasn't set when I came in yesterday. It didn't beep."

"So whoever took the laptop disarmed the alarm. Do a lot of people know the code?"

Sandy shook her head. "Just me and Tristan."

"Maybe the crime scene team didn't know how to arm it and didn't realize you weren't there."

"So someone's been in the house," Sandy murmured.

"Listen to me, Sandy. It could be nothing, but just to be on the safe side, maybe you should go into town and stay at the hotel, or go back to Baton Rouge."

"No," Sandy said. "This was probably some kid."

"Hold on a minute."

She heard Maddy talking to Zach, then suddenly the phone went silent. Maddy must have put it on mute. It didn't matter, because Sandy knew what they were saying. They were discussing whether there was still any danger to Sandy or anyone else in Bonne Chance.

"Maddy—" Sandy muttered. "Come on. Hurry up."

Finally Maddy unmuted her phone. "Sandy, if anything happens, call us, okay? We're not on the case anymore, but it hasn't been closed. So either Homeland Security or the NSA might reactivate it."

That quickly, the confidence that Sandy had in knowing that Homeland Security and the NSA had finished with Bonne Chance, the smugglers and Tristan's death drained away. "Why would they do that?"

Maddy hesitated—not for long, but it was long enough for Sandy to notice. "Maddy? You told me all the smugglers were arrested and the captain was killed by Boudreau. I thought that was the end of it."

"There are some things that we're not allowed to talk about. There are some things we're not even allowed to know."

"But you do know, don't you? I *knew* you and Zach weren't telling me everything. There's more to Tristan's death than you told me, isn't there?"

"Sandy, don't."

"Maddy, I swear I will come over there and wring your neck if you don't tell me what you know."

"Hang on a minute."

"No! Wait—" But Maddy was gone. Sandy waited impatiently. After about twenty seconds, she came back on the line.

"Sandy, listen carefully, because I can only say this

once. It's possible—just possible—that your husband's death was not an accident."

Sandy sat down. It was a good thing there was a chair right there. "What? So Zach was right? What happened? Is there some new evidence?"

"Listen to me. We spent a week in your house while we searched for answers to what happened to Tristan and all we could come up with was that his death was suspicious." Maddy took a breath. "So now Homeland Security is ramping up listening devices as well as working with the Coast Guard to do more spot inspections of the oil rigs. They're obviously worried that there may be another group out there that's planning something. Bonne Chance is probably one of the least populated and least noticed places on the Gulf Coast. It doesn't even have streetlights except on Main Street."

"I know. Out here, we can barely see lights from the town on clear nights, or if there's a fire we can see flames and smoke."

"Well, the darkness and isolation makes it desirable for smugglers."

"Maddy, you have to tell me why Zach—"

"Sandy!" Maddy snapped. "What did I just tell you?"

"A lot of vague stuff that you won't explain. Fine. I'll let you know if anything happens. That is if I'm able to." Sandy was being sarcastic, but Maddy had just laid a new and awful truth on her and refused to explain it.

Her husband may have been murdered.

"Sandy, call the sheriff and get him to take fingerprints off the desk. That's the easiest way to figure out who did it."

"If their prints are on file. But they probably aren't."

"Call the sheriff, Sandy," Maddy said.

"Maddy, this might not make any sense to you, but I don't want anyone in my house. I just got home. All I want to do is be here with the baby. We have a lot of things to sort out, him and me. There's no real reason to get fingerprints, is there?"

"Sandy, I mean it. I'm supposed to be in training this whole week, but I'll take a break and call you if I have to."

"All right. I'll call. Now can we talk about something else?"

"Sure. How are you feeling? Is the baby doing well?"

"Yes. We're both doing fine."

"Did that little thing ever fall off?"

"Little thing?" Sandy said. "Oh, right. That's what the doctor said about the sonogram. Not that I know of. It's still there."

"So did he actually say it's a boy?"

"No. Apparently physicians don't like to actually commit, but he sounded pretty sure. You know," she said with a sad smile, "Tristan said we were having a boy. He really believed it."

"Aw, honey."

"I know. Don't worry. I'm fine." Sandy forced a laugh.

"Have you thought of a name yet?"

"No. Not yet."

"So you're back there in Bonne Chance. Are you and the baby going to stay there?"

"I plan to," she said. "But I might go back over to Baton Rouge when I'm closer to the delivery date. It might be easier, having Tristan's mother to help me."

She barely listened as Maddy went on and on about what a great idea it was to go back to Baton Rouge. When she had a chance, she broke in and said goodbye, that she was going to sleep. Maddy warned her again what would happen if she didn't call the sheriff, then they hung up.

"Okay, bean. How about you? Do you think I should call the sheriff about the computer? Yeah. Me neither. Although I think I'll go see Boudreau tomorrow. Let him know I'm back. He might have seen someone sneaking around the house."

She smiled as she rubbed the side of her tummy. "Although, if Boudreau saw somebody he didn't know going into Tristan's house when I wasn't there, he'd probably shoot them."

Chapter Two

Tristan woke up feeling relaxed. The early-morning sun shone across his bed, warming his legs. He took in a deep breath, scented with gardenias. *Sandy.* She'd glowed the last time he'd seen her, just as a pregnant woman should.

As he smiled sleepily and turned toward her, searing pain tore through his calf, igniting painful memories.

He wasn't in his bed with his wife beside him. He was on a cot in his old Cajun friend Boudreau's cabin, where he'd been since Boudreau saved his life.

A memory of dark water and bright shark's teeth hit his brain. His muscles tensed and the hot pain in his calf, where muscle had been ripped away by thick, sharp teeth, seized him again.

Clenching his jaw and groaning quietly, he consciously relaxed his leg. He'd learned the hard way that if he could avoid tightening the tendons and whatever muscles were left on that side, it didn't hurt quite so bad.

The pain finally faded, but it was no relief. All he felt was a gaping emptiness inside. He was supposed to be dead. Was dead, as far as his hometown, Bonne Chance, Louisiana, and his family knew.

He couldn't have notified his family if he'd wanted to. According to Boudreau, he'd spent nearly two weeks unconscious, then when he finally woke up, he was too weak to stand and walk.

Since then, he'd forced himself to walk every day, pushing through the awful pain. He couldn't imagine how his mangled leg would ever work right, but if determination had anything to do with it, he would be successful.

Every morning, he sent up a prayer of thanks to God for letting him live. He'd been granted quite a few miracles in the past two months, and that one was the greatest.

He needed another miracle, though. He needed to walk across the dock from Boudreau's cabin to his family home. The miracle he envisioned was that once he got to the house, Sandy would be there waiting for him, beautiful and happy because he was alive.

He'd run to her without limping or falling and take her in his arms, feeling the swell of her tummy between them. She would take his hand and place it in just the right spot to feel their baby kick.

But Sandy wasn't there. She was in Baton Rouge with his mother, thank God.

Thank God for several reasons. First, while seeing her might be his fondest dream, that wasn't his primary motivation to recover as fast as he could. He had to find and bring to justice the man who'd ordered him killed.

And to do that, he needed to retrieve a vital piece of evidence—at least, he hoped it would be vital. But he had to get his hands on it and it was in the house.

As much as he longed for Sandy, he prayed she wouldn't come back to Bonne Chance. Not until he'd tracked down the person who had tried to kill him and wanted him dead.

While he'd been daydreaming about Sandy and their

baby, the sun had risen above the window casing. From the floor, he picked up the bumpy cypress walking stick Boudreau had whittled for him,

He took a deep, fortifying breath, then slowly sat up and swung his feet off the bed to the floor. Putting on his shoes was a painful chore, but not as painful as standing.

He used the stick to lever himself upright. As he balanced, putting weight on his right leg, he grimaced in anticipation.

And there it was. The pain. He cringed and tightened his grip on the walking stick. Outside, the morning sun shone through leaves and sent dappled shadows dancing across the ground.

Tristan lifted his face and let the energizing sun's heat soak through him, trying to keep his mind clear and open, trying to be glad he was alive.

But as hard as he tried to stay in the warm, bright present, the nightmare of his struggle with death clutched at him. He couldn't shake the memory of plunging into the dark, churning water off the oil rig.

He relived each terrifying moment, as dark, chill salt water seeped in through his mouth and nose and the shock of cold on his skin paralyzed his muscles.

He'd felt but hadn't reacted to the bumps and nibbles and flesh-ripping bites of the sharks that circled him until he'd opened his eyes and saw blood everywhere. His blood. It had swirled and wafted past him like ink dripped in water, darker than the brownish water of the Gulf.

Tristan gagged and coughed reflexively, and greedily sucked in fresh air until the horrible memories began to fade. He was beginning to appreciate the small things in life, like breathing. A wry smile touched his lips for a second as he limped over to a rough-hewn bench Boudreau had built under a pecan tree.

He didn't sit, because then he'd have to stand up again. Instead, he propped the walking stick against the bench and watched the morning come alive. Birds circled the yard, stopping to peck for seeds and nuts and insects.

Boudreau had a goat tethered to a tree with a generous amount of line so it could wander almost uninhibited. A vague memory of cool milk sliding down his throat took away the remembered burn of salt water.

As the quiet of dawn turned into the hustle and bustle of daytime in the bayou, Tristan made a decision. There was no more time for rest and recuperation. He had to solve the mystery of his near murder, and there was no better time than now. He would walk a mile today, all the way down to the dock and back. He was ready to walk that far. He had to be.

When Boudreau appeared, carrying a bucketful of water from a hidden artesian spring, Tristan told him his plan.

"What for you thinking about going down there?" Boudreau shook a finger at him. "You ain't got the stamina yet, you. You want somewhere to go? Strip the sheets off that cot and take them down to the spring and wash them. Use that Ivory soap. It don't hurt the water too much." He stalked past Tristan into the house and within a moment came back out, carrying the bucket, now empty.

"Haul up a bucketful of water when you're done washing. See how that goes, then we'll talk about how far you think you can walk."

"Boudreau," Tristan said. "You saved my life. If you hadn't been out fishing that morning and stopped the bleeding in my leg, I wouldn't be alive now. I owe you too much and respect you too much to argue with you, but I can't lie in bed any longer. I've got to strengthen this leg as much as I can, although I know it's never going to be as good as it was." He sighed. "There's enough I won't be able to do. I don't want it to wither down to complete uselessness."

"Wither? Son, ain't no use making up stories about what ain't happened yet. The future gonna happen, yeah, but its story ain't been writ yet. You start pushing yourself too much, you'll undo the good you've done and, before you know it, you'll accidently throw yourself into that future of your own making. See?"

"So what should I picture, rather than the truth that without most of the muscle in my calf, I'll never do better than a slow and painful limp for the rest of my life?" he asked bitterly.

Boudreau studied him for a moment. "How 'bout you picture that pretty little wife of yours back home and mourning for you. See if that's a better motivation."

"What? Sandy's back? Here?" Shocked, he glanced in the direction of the house. Then one of the many things Boudreau had told him during the past few weeks came into his mind.

He recalled his friend telling him that Murray Cho had gotten into the house without setting off the alarm and had come out a few moments later with what looked like Sandy's laptop computer.

Tristan had been surprised—he'd never imagined Murray Cho as a thief.

"She can't be back," he cried. "Murray could come back. He thinks she's gone, and if she surprises him—"

"There you go again, making a surefire mountain out

of a piece of ground where there might be a molehill one day. Slow down, son. Let things happen as they will. Just be ready when they do." Boudreau assessed him. "Meanwhile, how come you think she's not safe? You left her alone when you worked on the rigs."

He thought of Sandy, waiting for him week after week, never having a full-time husband, and he never having a full-time wife. Now she was less than a mile away.

He wanted to run to her and grab her up and kiss her until they both were panting with desire. He wanted to see how much her tiny baby bump had grown. And he wanted to put his hands on it and feel the child they had created, the child he already thought of as his son.

But he was afraid. Not only did he not want to show his face, he didn't want to chance her telling someone— her best friend, or his.

"I had no choice. Besides, I didn't know they were going to kill me. If they find out I'm alive, what's to stop them from doing it right this time?"

"Who's them? That captain's dead. Everybody's gone from the oil rig now."

"Come on, Boudreau. The captain was never the man in charge. The boss is still out there. He's some big muckety-muck in the company that owned the oil rig, Lee Drilling. And that man knows I can potentially identify him."

"Yeah?" Boudreau said. "Who is he?"

"I said *potentially*. I don't know who he is. The first time I heard the captain talking about a plan to smuggle illegal weapons into the US and give them out to kids on the streets, it was a complete accident. I realized I was listening to terrorists, and that was only one side of the conversation. I put together a program to capture and save every conversation that took place on that satellite phone."

"And that captain never said a name?"

"I don't know. I never had a chance to listen to all the recordings. Too afraid I'd get caught. I stored them on a flash drive, hoping I could get it to Homeland Security. They can use voice recognition technology to identify the man, and that will implicate him in the smuggling operation.

"Something went wrong with my program and the captain caught me fooling with his satellite phone. He kicked me out of his office and never said anything, but I know that's why they tried to have me killed."

"So where's that flash drive? You for sure didn't have nothing on you when I fished you out of the Gulf."

"That's just it. I hid it in the house the last time I was home. My plan was to get it to Homeland Security on my next week off. But I never got that week off. Now I don't know if Murray found it when he got the laptop."

"That's why you don't want Sandy back here."

Tristan nodded grimly. "I'd like to get Homeland Security to put a guard on her, but to do that, I'd have to let them know I'm alive. And as soon as they hear from me, they'll pull me in to DC for debriefing. Oh, they'd honor my request to guard her, but I can't be sure she's safe if I'm not the one protecting her. I mean look at how many good soldiers who have the protection of the government have been killed. How many innocent civilians."

"I get you wanting to protect her yourself, but, son, you ain't capable right now."

Tristan pinched the bridge of his nose. "So what are you saying? That my only choice is to notify Homeland Security? I'd be signing her death warrant. Somebody as high up as the captain's boss would know as soon as I surfaced. He'd have plenty of time to kidnap her before Homeland Security could react. She might end up being tortured for information she doesn't even have. And I wouldn't be here to rescue her."

SANDY FELT AS THOUGH she hadn't slept at all and therefore the little bean had been restless, too. She hadn't been able to shut her brain off. Every time she'd go to sleep, her dreams had been filled with images of Tristan sinking into the cold, dark water as hungry sharks circled around him. It was like a slideshow that wouldn't stop. *Click—murdered. Click—murdered. Click—murdered.*

Then she would wake up with her heart racing and tears wetting her cheeks and pillow.

Finally, around seven o'clock, she got up and bathed and dressed and headed into the kitchen. For a second, she stared at the coffeepot in longing. But she'd sworn off coffee for the pregnancy, not wanting to have a baby who was hooked on caffeine.

She yawned. "You have no idea how much I would enjoy a cup of coffee this morning. And there might be some decaf in the freezer. But my tummy has let me know in no uncertain terms that it likes grape juice and only grape juice." She patted her belly. "So grape juice it is, right?"

As she sat at the kitchen table and drank the juice, she looked at her phone, recalling Maddy's warning from the night before. She wanted to blow off the Homeland Security agent who had become her friend, but she knew Maddy would bug her until she called the sheriff. If she refused, Maddy would call him herself.

"No choice but to do it," she muttered as she got up

and went into the nursery. It was the only place in or out of the house where she could get a reliable cell signal. She dialed the sheriff's office.

"Baylor," she said when Sheriff Baylor Nehigh answered. "It's Sandy."

"Well, hello. I didn't know you were back in town," he said. "How're you doing? How's the baby?"

"Fine. We're fine," she said. "The baby's fine. Baylor—"

"Now how far along are you? I'm trying to remember."

Sandy closed her eyes and prayed for patience. If she couldn't get her question in, Baylor would be off on Tristan's death and she'd have to listen to his theories for at least twenty minutes before she could get another word in edgewise.

"Five and a half months, Baylor. I think someone got into the house while I was gone. My laptop computer is gone."

"Now, what? You say a computer is missing? Well, now, we can't be responsible for that. You'd have to talk to the crime scene unit, although my guess is that oil rig captain took it when he broke in to kidnap Agent Tierney," he said. "If it was him you'll never get any money for it."

"Baylor! That's not why I'm calling. The laptop went missing while I was gone. I thought if you or the crime lab had it then I don't need to worry that someone got into my house while I was away."

"I'll be glad to check on that for you, but do understand, my budget is too small to replace your laptop."

"I'm not asking you to. I'll buy a new one." She paused. "You don't want to take fingerprints or anything, do you?"

"I can send my deputy out there when he gets back.

It'll probably be after dark. He's gone to Houma to deliver some paperwork. I need a courier, but like I said—my budget won't handle it."

"No, no," Sandy said, feeling relieved. She didn't want anyone coming into her house right now. She'd come back to be alone with her baby and try to come to peace with Tristan's death. "I'm sure you're right about how it happened."

"Anything else I can do for you, Sandy?"

"No, Baylor. Thanks."

Sandy hung up while he was telling her to take care of herself. She rinsed her glass, then headed out to walk to Boudreau's cabin. She took a deep breath of clean morning air and yawned again. "I'm sorry about last night, bean. I couldn't get what Maddy said out of my head."

She wondered if talking to her unborn baby about things that upset her was bad for him. She hoped not, because talking to Tristan's child soothed her, and according to the latest baby books, it was good to let the baby become used to the mother's voice.

"Did you know your daddy was an undercover agent? Wait. What am I thinking? You were there when Zach told me. Naturally I had to hear it from his oldest friend, because Tristan apparently thought I didn't need to know that little tidbit." She heard the bitterness in her voice. She didn't want to sound like that when she talked about Tristan. Certainly not to her baby.

With an effort, she made her voice light and soft, the way she talked when she told him a fairy tale or quoted a poem. "He was a real-life spy, I guess. He worked for Homeland Security, catching bad guys. Until one day, one of the bad guys killed him."

She stopped talking because she had to. She was

breathing hard, mostly from trying not to cry, and she'd arrived at the dock. It was a beautiful morning. The sun glared and glistened off the water. "I should have gotten up earlier and watched the sunrise," she said wistfully. "Although without Tristan…" Her voice trailed off and she smiled sadly at the memories of sunrises and making love and being happy.

"Okay," she said briskly. "Let's go. I want to talk to Boudreau."

As she turned toward the path to Boudreau's cabin, she noticed slide marks in the mud. Stepping closer to the wooden pier, she studied the markings. Someone had pulled a boat up there since the last rain. She shook her head. It was probably Boudreau. He used the dock all the time.

"I've got to be careful," she murmured. "I'm seeing terrorists and bad guys everywhere."

The sun was already yellow and hot when she stepped out of the tangle of vines and branches into Boudreau's front yard. Boudreau was sitting on an old, rough-hewn bench, mending a tear in a fishing net.

"Well, now, you are moving much faster this—" he said, looking up. "What the hell you doing here?" he snapped, glaring at her.

"Boudreau, it's Sandy. Tristan's wife." He'd known her for years, and the last time she'd been here was on that awful night, when she'd come to tell him Tristan was missing and feared dead. But when he talked nonsense, like just now, she wasn't sure he remembered her.

Boudreau stood, dropping the fishing net and stalking toward her, the darning needle in one hand and his knife in the other. "I ask you a question. What you doing here? You go on now. Get out of here." He stopped, pointing the tip of the knife back the way she'd come. "Go!"

"But I need to talk to you. I want to close the dock—"

"Get out of here, Mrs. DuChaud. Get!" Boudreau shooed her as if he were shooing a chicken, with a sweeping motion of his hands. "Get!" he yelled again.

Sandy stared at him in openmouthed disbelief. This wasn't confusion. It was hostility. Did he think Tristan's death was her fault?

"Boudreau, please, listen to me. This is important."

He eyed her suspiciously. "I come down to your house one day soon. We talk then. Now you get out of here and back to your house *tout de suite* or I'll sic my dog on you, I guarantee."

She didn't know a lot about Boudreau except what Tristan had told her and he'd never mentioned the man being violent. But he had shot that oil rig captain in cold blood, so maybe the best thing to do was to leave.

"Please, come talk to me," she called out over her shoulder as she turned and headed back down the path she'd walked up to his shack.

"You just get gone and stay gone," she heard him say.

By the time she got to the dock she was breathing hard again, so she stopped for a few moments. She stood on the dock and looked out over the dark, greenish-gray waters of the Gulf of Mexico. And there, diving and surfacing as the sun glared off the water with such intensity it was difficult to see anything but the splashes and waves, was the creature that she'd seen the day before yesterday, frolicking in the water. She squinted and shaded her eyes, wishing she'd brought her sunglasses with her.

Nothing helped her see any better, though. The sun was higher now and the glare was too bright. And all at once, it seemed that whatever the creature was, it had sensed that she was watching, because the splashing stopped. Sandy blinked and put both hands up to deflect the sun, but the water was glassy and smooth and the sun reflected off it like a mirror.

Whatever—or whoever—had been playing in the water just beyond the shallows was gone now.

"I'm going to have to get up early one morning, bean, and get out here so I can catch whoever or whatever that is. Maybe it's a mermaid." She smiled and rubbed the side of her belly. "Or a merman."

Back at the house, she made herself some breakfast. By the time she'd finished eating, she'd convinced herself that Boudreau had shooed her away for her own protection. Maybe he knew there was a fox or a bobcat or an alligator running around that might do her harm. And he had promised to come see her. She knew from Tristan that if Boudreau said he would do something, he would.

"I guess we've got to wait for him, bean. He could have been nicer, though. He didn't have to yell like that. Kind of hurt my feelings." She drank the last of her juice and rinsed her glass and plate and set them on the drain board.

A glance at the clock told her it was just now eleven o'clock. "I still need to talk to him, though. He may have a better idea of how to keep people away from the dock," she told the baby. "He may already be guarding it. Maybe that *was* him I heard last night, checking to be sure no one was using the dock."

She yawned again. She'd been tired before she went to Boudreau's. "We've got to take a nap, bean. I'm about to fall asleep standing up. Then we've got to drive into Houma and get some groceries and buy me a new, smaller computer. A notebook. That'll be our big, exciting adventure for the day." As she said the words, a faint echo of a chill ran down her spine. "I hope," she added.

Chapter Three

It was almost dark when Sandy got back from shopping in Houma, which was twenty-five miles north of Bonne Chance, and if she'd been tired before, she was about to collapse from exhaustion now. She had stopped and bought a chocolate milk shake on the way. It was melted now, but she could put some ice in it and rejuvenate it a bit. Even melted, it sounded better than any of the food she'd bought at the grocery store. She was too tired to cook anything. Swallowing the melted shake would probably take the last of her strength.

She parked on the driveway just beyond the patio and grabbed her groceries and the new computer box in one hand and her house keys in the other. She was almost all the way across the patio to the door when she saw the footprints.

She nearly dropped the groceries. Automatically, she glanced around, but there was nothing to see. She stepped around the muddy tracks and tried the French doors. They were still locked.

She looked at the threshold, but there was no mud there. Relieved, she went inside and locked the doors behind her. Then she stood there and studied the muddy prints through the glass panes.

It was hard to tell how big or small the shoes were because the prints were smeared and the concrete was wet from an earlier rain. It looked as though they had no tread, though. So either the shoes were worn-out or they were soled in smooth leather.

Boudreau wore old, cracked leather boots. Maybe he'd walked over here while she was gone.

Of course, she thought with a sigh of relief. It was Boudreau who'd made the prints. It made her feel better that he'd come. Tristan had always told her that when he was away, Boudreau would watch over her.

She glanced at the clock on her phone. Eight o'clock. She stretched and yawned. "What do you think, bean? Too early to go to bed?"

She walked to the alarm box and set the door and window alarms, grabbed a glass of water and her milk shake, which she'd cooled with a couple of ice cubes, then headed into the master bedroom.

She'd already climbed into bed before she realized she'd left the curtains open. She didn't want to get up, but she certainly didn't want to sleep with the curtains like that, not after what had happened the last time she was here, when Murray Cho's son had spied on her.

She closed the curtains and climbed back under the covers. She picked up a book she'd begun at her mother-in-law's house, but it didn't take long for her to recall why she hadn't finished it before. She tossed it onto the floor and pulled an old fashion magazine from the shelf of the nightstand. It took practically zero concentration to glance through the ads and the fashion spreads.

She was nodding off over an ad for Bulgari earrings when the bean decided he was restless. "Ow!" she said. "Wow, bean. That was a good one."

She rubbed the place where he'd planted his tiny foot, not that it helped much. It was like scratching your thumb because your nose itched. The place that hurt was on the inside, so rubbing the outside, while it seemed like a good idea, didn't help much.

"Settle down. You're going to make me go to the bathroom again. Please don't kick my bladder." She grunted. "And there you go. That was my bladder. I'm so glad you mind well."

She stepped into the bathroom and saw that the curtains in there were open, too. She closed them, used the bathroom, then looked at herself in the mirror as she washed her hands. Her eyes were wide and dark.

"Come on, Sandy," she muttered. She looked like a pitiful heroine in a horror movie, although there was no reason to feel afraid in this house.

"This house is very safe," she said to the baby. "It's your daddy's house. It was his daddy's and his granddaddy's house. He promised me he would always keep me safe here. Me and you now." She felt tears starting up in her eyes and dashed them away angrily.

"This is Murray Cho's fault," she said. "It was his son, Patrick, who'd peeked in the window on the day of your daddy's funeral." She'd been terrified to see two men looking in her window, gaping into her private life.

"*Our* private life. I'm not sure I'll ever be the same." She sighed. "Not even when you get here," she said softly, patting her tummy where she thought his little back was. "It's their fault I'm scared."

She turned out the light and lay down, but there was no way she was going to fall asleep. It was just like the night before. Every time she closed her eyes, horrific visions haunted her. With a sigh, she sat up and turned on the lamp.

Opening the bedside table drawer, she picked up the prescription bottle and considered the label. *Take one or two for sleep.* She could take one. One would be safe. Extra safe, since the doctor had prescribed two.

She swallowed the pill with water. "Okay, let's try again," she whispered, then lay down on her side and cradled her pudgy tummy.

"Good night, little bean," she said as she felt something wet trickle down the side of her face to the pillow. "Why am I crying?" she grumbled out loud. She rarely cried and seldom ever needed help sleeping. But tonight, there was something bothering her and it wasn't the memory of two men peeking in her window.

She'd insisted on coming back here, had declared to Tristan's mother that she had to come back to the house where she and Tristan had lived together. She'd told her it was the only way she could heal. She'd meant it then, but now she wasn't so sure she'd made the best decision. An impossible thought had occurred to her while she'd been on the phone with Maddy. A ridiculous thought. A thought that couldn't possibly ever be true. But, whether it made sense or not, she couldn't get it out of her head.

What if it wasn't the Chos who had spawned this fear and dread that was keeping her from sleeping? What if it was the figure she'd seen at the window later on the night of Tristan's funeral? The figure that had to be a dream. Or was he? What if he'd been the one who'd taken her laptop computer?

Was it Tristan—or his ghost—that she was really afraid of?

She remembered him standing there just inside the

bedroom window, dripping wet, his face pale and haggard. Blood had dribbled down the side of his head, mixing with the water. Sandy shuddered. She never wanted to see that apparition again as long as she lived. She did not believe in voodoo. She did not believe in ghosts or demons or goblins—not on this earth. But she knew she couldn't live here if Tristan was going to keep showing up, even if he was just a figment of her grief-stricken imagination.

She knew he was only in her imagination, because if he were alive, he would never hurt her by pretending he was dead.

If Tristan were alive, he'd be here with her and their unborn baby.

TRISTAN UNLOCKED THE French doors of his home with the spare key that had been hidden in a fake flowerpot bottom for as long as he could remember. He shook himself, trying to get rid of the rainwater dripping off him.

Boudreau was right again. He'd been sure Tristan wasn't strong enough yet. Now, with his leg throbbing with pain and his head fuzzy with fatigue, Tristan had to agree. But he'd had no other choice.

Boudreau had told him about Sandy showing up at his cabin that morning while Tristan was swimming. But Tristan already knew she'd been out walking.

He'd gotten a glimpse of her at the dock from the water. She'd been shading her eyes and craning her neck, so the odds were that she couldn't see him because of the sun's glare. The fact that she hadn't shouted at him or marched back up to Boudreau's asking about him had been reassuring.

According to Boudreau she'd been agitated and nervous, as if she was afraid of something. And she'd seemed desperate to talk to him. But Boudreau, knowing that Tristan would soon be coming up the same path that Sandy would be walking down, had put her off and sent her home, hopefully in time to prevent them from running into each other.

Tristan made his way across the kitchen floor to the alarm control box behind the hall door, worrying about the squeaking of his sneakers. He disabled the alarm with two seconds to spare. He was way too slow.

He shook his head in disgust. He'd brought his walking stick with him, but he'd abandoned it by the French doors. He didn't want to use it inside the house and take a chance on dropping it or banging it into something.

He hobbled down the hall to the nursery, where he'd hidden the flash drive in plain sight. He'd thought at the time that he'd chosen an excellent hiding place. He had no idea how well it had worked, although he figured if anyone had found it, Boudreau would know.

So unless Sandy had noticed it, the device was probably still exactly where he'd put it. He'd grab it and go, and Sandy would no longer have anything that anyone wanted.

Of course, he'd have to figure out a way to assure the mysterious head of the terrorist group that had tried to smuggle guns, using his dock, that Sandy had no idea that he had been working undercover, nor was there anything in the house that could incriminate him.

But he would work that out later. Right now he just needed to get the drive and get out of the house without Sandy hearing him.

As he started to open the nursery door, he heard a

sound from behind him. He stopped dead still and listened.

Nothing. What had he heard, exactly? He reached for the knob and heard the same sound again. It was soft and low-pitched, and his heart wrenched when he realized what it was.

That was Sandy. He was sure of it. She was talking. It was almost two o'clock in the morning. She should be sound asleep. She was a lark, an early riser. She'd never stayed up past midnight or gotten up later than seven or seven-thirty. Although she *was* pregnant now, and he remembered his mom telling her that she'd be going to the bathroom almost constantly by the time the baby was born.

That was probably it. She'd gotten up to go to the bathroom. On the other hand, maybe she was talking or moaning in her sleep.

He waited, listening. He was in no hurry. Once she settled down he could sneak out without her ever knowing he'd been there.

He stood there on his left foot, flexing the right, trying to stretch and exercise the muscles that were left beneath the ugly scar where Boudreau had stitched up the gaping wound. Point then flex. Point then flex.

After a few moments without a sound, he turned the knob again. He was just about to push the door open and slip into the nursery when he heard a familiar sound that twisted his aching heart even more. The sound of Sandy's bare feet on the hardwood floor. Then the knob on the master bedroom door turned. Within the couple of seconds while he wondered if he had time to push the door open, slip through and ease it shut, the master bedroom door opened and his wife stepped through it into the hall.

In the dim glow of a night-light from the kitchen, he saw that she had on pajama pants and a little sleeveless pajama top that stretched over an obvious baby bump. She'd hardly been showing at all the last time he'd seen her.

He stared at her smooth, rounded belly barely covered by her pajama top. He wanted to touch it, to kiss it, to feel the movements of the tiny little child growing inside. He had missed her so much, and here she was, close enough that he could reach out and take her into his arms, and he couldn't.

If she knew he was alive, she would be furious—more than furious—that he'd let her believe he was dead. She wouldn't understand the danger. She'd spent her entire life in the belief that just because he was with her, she was safe.

That was the one thing about her that had always awed him.

Sandy had always believed in him.

He just prayed that she loved him enough to forgive him for this unforgivable hurt he'd caused her.

She yawned and pushed her fingers through her hair, leaving it sticking out in tangled waves all over her head. He smiled. He knew her, knew her every move, her every little gesture. She was three-quarters asleep, padding on autopilot to the kitchen in her bare feet. Her habit of getting a drink of water without ever completely waking up might save him if he stood perfectly still. Often, people only noticed things that moved.

He concentrated on keeping his bad leg still. If he tensed it too much, the muscles jerked involuntarily. "It's okay," she whispered.

Shock flashed through his body like lightning and instantly the muscles in his right leg cramped. He clenched his jaw. Was she talking to him? He couldn't move. Didn't dare.

"Ow. Watch it, bean. I know I woke you up. I just need some ice for my water and maybe a couple of crackers. Kinda nauseated," she murmured, rubbing the side of her belly. "Then we'll get back in bed."

She wasn't talking to him. She was talking to her baby. To *their* baby. Tristan's eyes stung. It hurt his heart to know how much he had missed. He'd been gone too much, working on the oil rig for two weeks or more at a time, and he'd missed most of the pregnancy. And now… now she thought he was dead.

He held his breath as she took her first step up the hall. There was no way she could pass by without seeing him. He debated whether he should speak to her or wait and let her notice him on her own. Which would be less traumatic?

Sandy jerked as the baby's foot knocked the haze of sleep right out of her head. "Oh, why do you have to kick, bean," Sandy said, rubbing her belly. "One day your foot's going to kick right through—"

She gasped and stopped cold. What was that? Her heart suddenly vied with the baby's foot to see which could burst through her skin first. She pressed her fist to her chest.

Dear God help her. There was someone there. In the dark. Right in front of her. Her first instinct was to turn and run, but she couldn't move. Her arms and legs were numb with fear.

"Who are you? Wh-what do you want?" she asked, trying to force a cold sternness into her voice, but hearing it quaver.

The dark shadow didn't move. She took a step backward as the nausea that had woken her hit her again. She felt hot and cold and terrified.

"Get out," she said hoarsely, then filled her lungs and shrieked, "Get out! Get out now!" She ran out of breath too fast. Her heart was drumming against her chest wall now. *Boom-boom run! Boom-boom run! Boom-boom!*

"Sandy," a voice that could not possibly be speaking said.

She recoiled, her back slamming against the wall. Her throat closed up. Her lungs burned with the need for oxygen. Another scream built behind her throat, but when she opened her mouth all that escaped was a quiet squeak.

She pressed her hands flat against the wall behind her, as if she could make it move, and dug her heels into the hardwood floor, trying to get away from the thing that was hovering in front of her. "Oh, please," she whispered desperately. "Come on, Sandy, wake up. *Stupid dream.*"

"San, you're not asleep," the voice said gently. "Don't be afraid."

She tried one more time to get air past her strictured throat into her lungs, but she couldn't. Her fingers curled at her constricted throat, then stars danced before her eyes and the next thing she knew, she was crumpled on the floor and the wet, haggard ghost from her nightmare was crouching above her, dripping water on her and calling her name.

"I'm asleep," she muttered. "In bed, asleep."

"You're not asleep," a familiar voice said softly.

"No, no, not again," she whispered, shaking her head back and forth. Then she felt a wet hand on her cheek and she squealed and propelled herself backward as fast and hard as she could, but she was already up against the wall.

"No!" she cried. "No, no. Get away."

"Sandy, listen to me. I'm sorry. I'm so sorry. I didn't mean to scare you."

She felt his hand and the soft whisper of his breath against her cheek. Water dripped down his pale, drawn face, just as it had in her dream.

She understood now that on the night of his funeral what she'd seen had been a dream. He'd hovered by the same window where Patrick Cho had peeped in on her. But unlike Patrick, Tristan had been insubstantial, a shimmering awful specter that had dissolved into nothing as she'd watched.

Tonight he was not dissolving. She touched his face. "Tristan?" she whispered. "You're real." It wasn't a question.

The water dripping off his hair and clothes was wet on her skin. The face she was touching was sickly white, yes, but it was warm and fleshy and, most important, it was not fading before her eyes. She grabbed a handful of his hair and squeezed it. Her hand came away soaking wet. She looked at it and laughed, but the laugh turned into a sob.

His brown eyes turned darker. "I'm real," he said, his mouth stretching into a wry smile as a dampness glistened in his eyes.

She sobbed again and put her hand over her mouth, hoping to stop the hiccuping sobs before they stole what little oxygen she had left in her lungs.

"It's okay, San. It's okay."

"How—" She reached out to touch him, hesitated,

then gingerly touched his shoulder. It was firm, strong, alive. Oh, dear God.

She met his gaze and found him watching her intently. He didn't try to pull her close or hug her, and she was fine with that.

He was here, and his hair was dripping with real water and his face was damp. But there was a part of her that was afraid to trust her own eyes and ears and fingers. She looked at her hand, then back at him.

"San? It's okay," he said again. "It's me."

The voice. The eyes. "It is you," she said. "How? Shouldn't you be dead?"

"Almost was," he muttered. "How're you doing? How's—"

"But where?" she broke in. "Where have you been? Where did you go? It's been two months!"

"Boudreau found me. He's been taking care of me."

"Boudreau? You mean you've been right over there all this time?" She dug her heels into the hardwood floor to push away from him.

"We. Buried. You. We had a funeral. We cried. We mourned you. I thought I was going to die because I would never see you again. And you were *less than a mile* away the whole time?" She pushed at his chest and he almost toppled over. He caught himself with a hand to the floor just in time.

"Sandy, it's okay."

"Okay?" She laughed hollowly. "You think so? I wake up in the middle of the night and find my dead husband sneaking into my home and looking cornered when I run into him. What the hell are you doing here?"

Suddenly, the floodgates opened in her mind. Thoughts and questions whirled around in her head so fast that she could barely speak. As soon as she started to demand one answer, another question pushed its way to the forefront, insisting on being asked. A still shot of memory flashed across her inner vision.

The casket at the open door of the DuChaud vault as Father Duffy deliberately turned her away from the sight and asked her a distracting question.

She stared at him in horror, her mouth turning dry with trepidation. "Who was in there?" She pressed a hand to her lips. "Who's in the vault? Who's…buried in—" she giggled a bit hysterically "—in Tristan's tomb?" She hiccuped.

Tristan stared at her for a brief moment. "My…tomb?" he echoed, as if the fact that a casket was placed in the DuChaud family tomb had never occurred to him. "I don't know," he said, his eyes burning like dark fire.

Then he sat back, put his hands on the floor and maneuvered his left foot under him. She could barely see his face, which was in profile to her, but his jaw tensed and he bared his teeth as he used just his left foot and his hands to push himself to his feet.

She watched and realized why he'd almost toppled over when she'd pushed him.

"Oh, my God," she whispered.

He finally got himself upright. He stood with his head bowed, his breaths sawing loudly in his throat. He flattened a palm against the wall to steady himself. In the dark, his pale face floated above his dark clothes like a disembodied head.

"What happened to you?" She was still sitting with her back to the wall. She pushed herself to her feet, murmuring to her little bean encouragingly as she stood.

"It's okay, bean. You're fine. I'm fine." She looked

up, realizing that her fear and panic had drained away and the only thing left inside her was anger, rising to the surface like a bubble in a lake.

"Tristan? Talk to me," she said through gritted teeth.

He glanced at her sidelong. "Sorry, San. It's a long story." He huffed. It could have been a chuckle, except that his expression didn't change. "A very long story," he mumbled.

The bubble burst and fury washed over her like a red tide. This was Tristan, standing in front of her. He was real. And he'd been alive. All this time, he'd been alive. "A long story? That's your answer?"

She realized that the anger felt good. It didn't weigh on her like grief and sorrow. It invigorated her. She clenched her fingers into fists. Her husband was alive and she was pissed off.

He glanced at her for an instant, then looked away. "I didn't mean to wake you up. I should have been in and out of here in, like, two minutes."

"In and out?" she echoed.

He spread his hands. "I don't know where to start. It's—"

"A long story. Yeah. I got that," she said. "Not a problem, *sweetheart*. I've got all night."

Chapter Four

Ten minutes later, Sandy sat at the kitchen table, clutching a rapidly cooling mug of decaf coffee that her husband, who was supposed to be dead, had made for her.

It was a cliché, but she really did feel as though she'd walked into a play where everyone knew their lines except her. In fact, she was reminded of a movie about a man whose entire life was a TV show, and he was the only one who thought it was his real life. She almost glanced around to see if she could spot hidden cameras.

Across from her, Tristan sat, staring into his mug. She studied him as long as she could, which was only a few seconds, then looked away. If she looked at him for longer, it did awful, painful things to her insides.

But his tortured expression wasn't the worst thing. Nor was the fact that he looked so tired and sick she couldn't believe he was upright. It wasn't even that she could feel his pain. No. The worst thing was that her heart and head and gut throbbed with anger at him.

"You said if I hadn't gotten up you'd have been in and out in a few minutes."

Tristan glanced up. "I did?"

"You know you did. What were you doing here? Obviously you didn't come to tell me that you are still alive and doing fine."

He looked down. "I had to get something," he muttered.

"What? Tris, look at me."

"I said I had to get something. San—"

"Don't San me. When exactly did you think you'd let me know that you didn't *die*?"

"Look, I'm sorry, but there are other things to consider here."

"Other things? *Other things?* You mean than letting your wife know you're alive? Or coming home to your unborn child? If I had any sense I'd kill you myself, right now."

His gaze flickered downward to her tummy and an expression of longing and sadness crossed his face. Sandy almost reached out to him, but then he looked away and muttered something she couldn't understand.

"Would you speak up? What did you just say?"

He waved a hand. "Nothing." He went back to staring into his mug.

"I think I hate you," she said, her voice as flat and cold as an iceberg. It made her shiver. She squeezed the mug more tightly, until her fingers ached.

Tristan nodded sagely. "Trust me, San, I know." He lifted his mug to his lips, then frowned and set it down. "I kinda hate me, too."

"Well, you should." Sandy stood. She couldn't look at the changing expressions on his face. If she did she'd start feeling sorry for him and that would lead to feeling other things and she was not about to get sucked back into the evocative vortex of loving Tristan. She couldn't. Not now, when he'd proven that, even after a lifetime of love, he wasn't the trustworthy protector she'd always depended on.

She picked up his mug and took it to the sink along with hers. With her back to him, she blinked and looked up, trying to force the tears to flow backward, back to where they came from. But as usual, they were determined to fall. She rinsed the mugs and then splashed cold water onto her face.

Picking up a dish towel, she turned around and leaned back against the counter. Water she'd splashed onto the countertop seeped into her pajamas, wetting her lower back and sending a chill through her.

"So, wh-where have you been?" she stammered. It was the first question she wanted to ask and the last answer she wanted to hear.

She was dying to know, but she knew when he told her it was going to break her heart.

At the same time, a sickening dread told her she didn't have to wait to find out. She already knew what he was going to say. All this time, while she mourned him and ached for him and lay in her lonely bed, he was less than a mile away, at Boudreau's.

She waited for him to tell her that, but he didn't answer. He stood and limped over to stare out the French doors.

Sandy tried not to compare him with the man she'd last seen three months ago when he'd left for his monthlong work shift on the *Pleiades Seagull*. That man had been irritating, grouchy and depressed, but he'd been healthy and handsome and sun-browned despite the sunscreen she tucked into his duffel bag every time he headed back out to the oil rig. His hair had been streaked with golden-blond highlights put there by the sun, his shoulders had been broad and he, for all his faults, had been the man she knew and loved better than anyone in the world. The man she'd always known she could trust.

This person, although he sported Tristan's blazing dark brown eyes, straight nose and wide mouth, was not him. When that thought hit her, she sobbed. It was a small hiccup that barely made a sound, but Tristan's head turned toward her.

She put a hand over her mouth. That stiff, strong back, the lines of pain that scored his face from his nose to his chin, told a story of horror that she had not been a part of nor could ever understand. And that horror, those two long months of suffering, had changed him. His dark eyes were wide and too bright above sunken cheeks and pinched nostrils. His hair was too long, mousy brown and lifeless.

His back was ramrod straight, with a desperate dignity she'd never seen in him before. He'd lost at least fifteen pounds, maybe more, from a frame that had always been lean.

Her gaze traveled down his straight back and she pressed her hand hard against her lips and teeth, swallowing another sob. The pants he wore were too big, held up by a belt that had been tightened to the very last hole. The material was cotton and soaking wet, so it clung revealingly to his thighs and calves. She could see exactly what had happened to his right leg. Beneath the material, the right calf was no more than half the size of his left.

She remembered what Zach had told her about the strip of calf muscle that had been recovered from the water and identified as coming from Tristan's body. Just one of the several things that had convinced the authorities that Tristan could not have survived.

Sudden nausea, hot and sour and insistent, swept over her. She barely had time to turn to the sink before she threw up. It took forever for her stomach to stop heaving and spasming.

When she was done and had rinsed her mouth with a handful of water, she reached for the dish towel. With a shuddering moan, she dried her face and held the towel against it until she was certain that the spasms were dying down and she wouldn't gag anymore.

When she turned around and lowered the towel, Tristan was facing her. His face wasn't just ghostly—it had turned a sickly shade of green.

"Are you okay?" he asked.

She nodded.

His gaze dropped to her swollen belly. "You still have morning sickness?"

She shook her head.

"But—" he gestured vaguely.

"That? Oh, I don't know. Maybe a combination of no dinner, finding an intruder in my house and seeing my dead husband."

"How's—" His hand reached out, but stopped in mid-air. He stared at her baby bump, looking slightly bewildered.

"The baby?" she said, irritation rising and pushing the nausea away. "The baby is fine."

"San? I didn't mean for this to happen. I wasn't— I couldn't—" He stopped. Moving awkwardly, he stepped close to her. He lifted a hand and brushed her hair away from her forehead.

His hand was surprisingly warm, given his drenched state. Her head inclined naturally toward it. "Oh, Tris, I missed you so," she whispered.

He bent his head and pressed his forehead against hers. "I'm so sorry," he said, then pulled back. "Is it okay if I touch you?"

"You want to feel the baby?" she asked. "He kicks all the time these days."

Tristan gingerly laid his palm against her swollen tummy. Again, she was surprised at how warm it was.

He stood there, his hand caressing her belly, for a long time. "I can't believe it's been two months," he murmured.

Immediately, her anger swelled again. She pushed his hand away. "Two months in which I mourned you and thought I'd have to live the rest of my life without you. And if you'd had your way, I'd still think you were dead. I can't believe you came here and expected to leave without waking me."

She drew a shaky breath. "I don't understand why you didn't want to see me. To tell me you were alive. My husband would have crawled here if he couldn't walk, to let me see him and know that I had not lost the love of my life. My husband would not have made me grieve and mourn and hurt for two months."

"San, listen to me," Tristan said. "I was unconscious—"

"That is no excuse. What about Boudreau? Why didn't he come and tell me? A true friend of my husband would have let me know." She sucked in a harsh breath.

"Don't blame Boudreau."

"So, that is where you've been all this time? Right across the dock at Boudreau's cabin, less than a mile away? Oh, get out! Get out of here!" she cried, knowing as the words left her mouth that she didn't mean them.

Tristan stepped backward, away from her. He stared

at her for a moment, then nodded to himself as if he'd made a decision or come to a realization.

He smiled, but that wasn't aimed at her, either. It was the subtlest, saddest smile she'd ever seen. It made her want to cry, to go to him and take him in her arms and promise him that everything was going to be fine, even though she knew it wasn't.

Just about the time she'd decided he was too sick and wounded and in too much pain to be sent out to make his way back to Boudreau's, he turned and twisted the knob on the French doors and opened them.

"Tristan?" she said hoarsely. "Where are you going?"

He turned to look at her. "Back to Boudreau's," he said.

"Fine. Go. Stay there."

Awkwardly, he bent over and picked up a carved walking stick that she hadn't noticed on the floor beside the doors.

Once he had the stick and was leaning on it, he raised his gaze to her. "You said he."

"What?"

"You said *he* kicks all the time. The baby's a boy?"

His face was suddenly so filled with hope and longing that she thought her heart would shatter. "That's what the doctor said."

"A boy," he repeated, his voice tight. He turned back toward the door.

"You're still going?" she asked, surprised.

He didn't answer. He just stepped through the French doors and headed toward the overgrown path.

HE'D WALKED OUT. Now if he could just keep going. He hadn't wanted to leave. What he'd wanted to do was hold his wife, breathe in the sweet, familiar scent of her hair and touch her petal-soft skin.

He wanted her to wrap her arms around him and welcome him back. But even more than that, he'd wanted to lay his palms on her tummy and feel their baby—their son.

But she'd been so angry and hurt. He could not, would not, force himself back into her life.

He walked slowly and awkwardly across the patio and onto the slippery wet grass in the yard, hoping he could make it out of her sight before he collapsed from pain and fatigue.

There was no way he could make it over to Boudreau's cabin.

He heard Sandy's voice behind him.

"Could you come back in here, please?" she asked harshly. "You can't get up that hill tonight. Not with your leg in that condition. And even if you could, it's pitch-dark out there. You're liable to slip and end up drowning in gumbo mud. I don't want to be responsible for you *really* dying this time."

"You're not responsible for me," he yelled. "So don't worry about it."

"Not re—" She laughed bitterly. "What about those vows? Did they mean nothing? Of course I'm responsible for you. You're my husband. I—"

Tristan knew what she'd been about to say. *I love you.* But she hadn't been able to force out the words. That disturbed him. She'd never been shy about saying it. She'd sung it in the middle of church one Sunday when they were around ten years old. She'd written it on the chalkboards in their classes several times every school year.

And she'd had it printed on a huge banner that hung suspended over the pulpit on the day of their wedding.

So it was ominous that she couldn't bring herself to say it on the night that her dead husband reappeared, alive and well—or almost well.

"Okay, then," she said, apparently taking his silence for agreement. "Get in here and let's get you settled in. Maybe you'd be comfortable in the guest room," Sandy said. "That way—"

"Wait a minute. I didn't say I'd stay." He couldn't spend the night anywhere close to her. Just a few whiffs of her hair had nearly driven him crazy.

His calf muscle cramped and the leg nearly gave way, a not-so-gentle reminder that no matter what he wanted, how much he longed to be close to her, no matter what seeing her did to him, the simple truth was that in his current condition, even if he wanted to make love with her, even if she invited him to, he couldn't. He was still weak, and his leg couldn't take the workout involved.

He shook his head and opened his mouth to tell her that he was fine and that walking through the overgrown paths that led to Boudreau's house wasn't a problem, but at that instant it began to rain hard. He grimaced.

"Well, you can't go now," she said ungraciously. "The ground will be even more slippery."

"I've got to get back. I need—" He stopped himself. He'd almost told her he needed the concoction that Boudreau had brewed up. It was a mixture of natural herbs and substances. According to Boudreau it had a natural painkiller, natural immune-system boosters and something to help him sleep. Without realizing on a conscious level that he'd moved, he found himself walking back across the patio and through the French doors.

Sandy handed him a towel. He took it while continuing to protest.

"Boudreau needs me," he said and saw in her face that she didn't believe him for a second.

"Boudreau needs *you*," she stated wryly. "He needs you? Come on, Tris, don't give me that. *I'm looking at you.*" Sighing, she spread her hands in a supplicating gesture. "There was a time I believed every word you said. And it wasn't that long ago."

Tris saw her eyes begin to shine more brightly.

"Sandy, don't complicate this. I haven't been on my feet but a few days. There was no big conspiracy to keep me hidden. Certainly not from you. I came here as soon as I could walk this far."

She stared at him, shaking her head. "Right. You already told me you came here to get something. You probably thought I was still in Baton Rouge."

He shook his head. "No. I told you. It's very simple. Boudreau told me you were back."

"Damn it, Tristan, you're doing what you've always done. You're simplifying the situation beyond belief. You're acting like we're nine years old and you're trying to convince me that my dad won't hit me if I just go on and tell him it was me who dented the car with a baseball, if he's not drinking. Trouble is he was never not drinking. So you were wrong about that and you're wrong about his. You let me think you were dead. This can't be solved with a little strip bandage or a kiss from Mommy or a great, big *I'm sorry, pumpkin* from Daddy Dearest."

"Really, San? You think I'm oversimplifying anything? Look at me. Look. At. Me." He reached for her arm.

She recoiled, her eyes wide.

"You really believe that I think a little bandage will solve anything? You know me better than that. Or at least I thought you did. But you were never happy that I went to work on an oil rig, were you? You thought you were going to get a veterinarian and all you got was a blue-collar worker."

"I did hate you working offshore. And it was bad enough when you were just working there. When you started working for Homeland Security and were not only gone all the time, but distracted and worried when you were here, I hated it more."

He was surprised and she saw it in his face.

"That's right. I figured out what you were really doing on that rig. I don't understand why you couldn't tell me, but I can respect that you had to keep it secret. But letting me believe that you died? That was low." She studied him and her big blue eyes filled with tears. "Great, now I'm crying."

Tristan almost smiled. It didn't matter what was going on—wedding, funeral or silly movie, Sandy cried.

"I see that. I'm a little surprised, though. This isn't exactly a Hallmark commercial." He winced internally when he heard the sarcastic tone in his voice.

Her jaw tensed and she glared at him. "No. It's real life and it's not going away. We still need to talk about it."

"Talk about it?" His tone grated. "You mean like this? This isn't talking. You want to talk? Let's talk about this—you going back to Baton Rouge and staying with my mom. You'll be safe there."

"Safe? From what?"

"Did you miss the part where somebody tried to kill me? Or here's an idea. You and Mom should go somewhere, then. Somewhere nobody can trace you. Maybe

go to DC and stay with Zach until I can clear all this up."
He liked that idea. His old friend from childhood who'd
become an NSA undercover agent would know how to
keep them safe.

But Sandy's instant anger told him that he'd made another mistake. He could almost see smoke coming out
of her ears.

She put one hand on her little baby bump and raised
the other, her index finger pointing at him. "You're crazy
if you think I am going to go away somewhere and leave
you with Boudreau to take care of you."

"He's done okay so far," Tristan interjected.

"What? Look at you. You can barely walk. You're at
least fifteen pounds—maybe more—underweight. Just
where is the good job he did?"

"Right here." Tristan jabbed a thumb into his chest.
"Right here. If it hadn't been for him I would be dead
now."

Her eyes widened for an instant. "Oh, please, Tris.
He's crazy and he's Cajun. That in itself is a lethal combination. What did he do? Give you a potion, then touch
your forehead and say, 'Stand up and walk, I guarantee'?"
Her tone was bitter as she mocked Boudreau.

She had the potion right, but what Boudreau had said
was *You get your own self up and go swim. Or your legs
gonna be withered and you be crawling around like a
cripple the rest of your life, you.*

"What he did that saved me was not waste time trying
to get me to a doctor or a hospital." Tristan cut a hand
through the air. "Never mind. You're not going to believe
a word I say right now, are you?"

"No, I'm not. You lied to me and that means you're

a lying liar. So no. I'll be assuming from now on that if your mouth is open, you're telling me a lie."

Tristan wiped his face with an unsteady hand.

"And look at you," she said. "If you don't get some real care, real medications and real cleansing and bandaging of those wounds, you could die of...of sepsis or infection." Her voice cracked as she continued to fight tears. "Why can't *you* go to DC? Why can't you tell Zach everything and let him protect you?"

Tristan shook his head. "Have you not heard a word I've said? I. Am. Not. The. Only. One. In. Danger. Should I repeat that, so you're clear?"

"Oh, I'm clear," she snapped. "I'm starting to see a lot of things clearly that I never saw before."

"Sandy—" Tristan started.

Sandy held up her hand. "Okay, then. We can both go, together. I'll drive."

But he was already shaking his head. "That doesn't work. If we do that, they'll get Boudreau."

"Then we can take him with us."

"Right. Take Boudreau. Besides, don't you think they know who Zach is by now? Just listen to me. Boudreau and I are going to work something out."

Sandy growled. "Ooooh, you've just got an answer for everything, don't you?" She clenched her fists. *"Everything."*

He couldn't help but stare at her. She was furious and he was so frustrated he could almost be tempted to wring her pretty neck, but when she got mad her eyes sparkled like sapphires, her cheeks turned a nice shade of pink and her hands wrapped protectively around her stomach. His heart felt as though it would burst with love for her and the baby.

"What are you staring at?" she snapped. "Could you try to help me come up with something? There has to be an answer."

Then suddenly, for no apparent reason, all the discussion and planning and rejecting of plans that he and Boudreau had been doing coalesced and he had it. He looked at her thoughtfully. "There is an answer," he said.

"Well, then, tell me. Why have you been beating around the bush—" She frowned at him. "Wait a minute. What are you talking about?"

But he didn't have to answer. She was already putting it together.

"Oh, no," Sandy said, shaking her head. "No, no, no! You are *not* setting yourself up as bait. They'll kill you."

"San, this is not a discussion and it's not up for a vote. It's the only way I can stop them."

"I said no!"

But Tristan didn't hear the word *no*. It was drowned out by a deafening explosion.

Chapter Five

Sandy shrieked involuntarily, but she couldn't hear herself. The explosion was too loud. It took her a fraction of a second to realize that the thunderous crash had actually been thunder. She remembered a quick, bright flash of light right before the noise.

Now, at least for the moment, the sky was dark and the explosion of thunder was fading to a deep rumble. In the suddenly dark kitchen, Sandy felt disoriented.

She lost her balance and fell against Tristan, who almost toppled. He caught himself against the facing of the French doors as she scrambled to get her feet under her and push away from him. But his arms slid around her and tightened and everything changed.

He held her tightly against him and all the things about him that she'd missed were right there, molded to her body, just as they should be. His strong arms, his warm broad chest and his chin, under which her head fit perfectly.

She slid her arms around his waist, trying not to think about how fragile he felt, with ribs sticking out on his sides and back. All she wanted to do was bury herself in him and drink in his familiar scent, and the hard-planed muscles under his smooth skin.

She turned her head and pressed her lips against his collarbone. "Tris," she whispered, "I missed you. I missed this so much."

He took a sharp breath. "Sandy, I—" He let go of her and stared through the glass panes of the doors. Just at that instant, lightning flashed again.

"Get down," he growled.

"What? What is it?" she asked.

"Keep your head down and go into the living room!" His hand raised, pointing, silhouetted by a flash of lightning.

She bent over and crept away from the French doors and into the living room. "What did you see?" she whispered.

"Shh," he said, cutting the air with his flattened hand.

Sandy waited, both irritated at his orders and grateful that he was there. Whatever he'd spotted in the flashes of lightning, she was glad she didn't have to face it on her own.

It was about five minutes before he came into the living room, massaging his forehead with his fingertips.

"Well?" she said. "What was out there?"

"Nothing. A trick of the lightning."

"Liar! Lying liar!" Sandy pulled herself upright by grabbing the door frame. "You expect me to believe that you acted like that over some waving branches? You used to play outside in thunderstorms."

He shrugged. "I'm just telling you what I saw. Something looked a little odd, but I never saw it again."

"Tristan, stop it, please. You're acting—I don't know— different. I know you saw something, or somebody, out there. Why can't you tell me like you always have, and we'll deal with it together."

"I'm not different. It's the situation. Someone tried to kill me. That same person wants to smuggle automatic handguns into the US. I'm the only one who even has a chance of identifying him. But, Sandy, I promise you. Nothing has changed. I'm still the same person I always was."

"N-nothing has changed?" she sputtered, as her tears changed to a bitter laughter. "You…can't be…serious!" she gasped, laughing. "Maybe you think you haven't changed, Tristan, but everything, *everything*, around you has. You may still live in the same world as before you fell overboard, but I don't. Did I tell you the rest of it? Did I tell you that they told me they'd found parts of your body that the…sharks didn't eat?"

She could barely repeat the words the ME had told her.

Tristan stood without moving, his face averted. She kept going. "I had to pick out a casket and talk to Father Duffy about a service. I had to choose flowers for the top of the casket." She stopped to take a deep breath.

"Do you understand what I'm saying? Do you get that *you were dead*? I had nothing to hold on to. No hope. *Nothing!*" She was almost out of control and she knew it. She had to calm down, for the baby's sake. He was wriggling and kicking, upset because she was upset.

"Sandy, I never meant—"

She held up her hands. "No!" she snapped. "I can't do this anymore. Just leave," she said brokenly. "Leave!"

"I'm not leaving. I don't know what I saw, but I'm not taking any chances."

"I knew it," she said flatly. "I knew you saw more than a branch. At this point, I feel more capable of facing whoever is out there than you. And you're upsetting the baby." She pressed her hand against the side of her belly where the bean's little foot was.

"Do whatever you want to. I don't care as long as I don't have to…look at you." She turned on her heel and stalked down the hall to her bedroom with as much dignity as she could muster.

THE BEDROOM DOOR SLAMMED. Tristan spat a curse in Cajun French and slammed the heel of his palm into the door facing. He cursed again when his hand throbbed with pain. "Ow. *Fils de putain*—" He clamped his jaw, shook his hand and tried to get his anger under control.

In one way, he understood why Sandy was so angry at him. When his dad died right before his high school graduation, he'd been furious and terrified. As much as he'd hated his father's job, he had loved his father. But with him gone, Tristan had known that the future he'd hoped to have as a veterinarian was impossible. He'd had to drop out of school and take a job on the oil rigs, just like his old man.

His family was there, too, with all the churning emotions Sandy had described. The only difference was that his dad hadn't shown up later.

She'd had to experience the trauma and grief of finding out he was dead, and then the equally traumatic experience of finding out he was alive. Of course she'd be angry, at least at first.

He was angry, too.

There had been a time, not too long ago, when he'd have sworn that he and Sandy had never and would never have a serious fight. They'd known each other practically all their lives and had learned long ago that they were perfectly suited for each other.

But then he'd started keeping secrets. He'd never told her about his job with Homeland Security. He'd lied to her and he'd pretended he was dead.

Lightning was still flashing in the sky, fainter than before. Tristan took a step closer to the door and looked out. There wasn't as much rain and he wasn't hearing thunder anywhere. The storm was over.

Of course, he knew as well as Sandy that it would be days before their electricity came back on. Meanwhile, at least they had candles and a camping stove. They were in the laundry room, just off the kitchen.

Before he could start in that direction, he saw something move outside. He froze. It was a larger shadow among the smaller, darker ones out beyond the patio. The shadow was noticeable because it was moving, not just quivering as the raindrops hit the leaves or swaying in the shifting wind.

His muscles tensed, but he remained perfectly still, his eyes straining as he stared at the shadow, waiting for it to move again.

He stole a glance into the living room, where his dad had kept a pair of guns hanging above the fireplace. One was a double-barreled shotgun and the other was some kind of rifle.

Tristan didn't like guns. Never had, not even when he was a kid and almost all of his friends wanted to play cops and killers.

He stared at the two weapons now, trying to decide which one he could carry more easily. The rifle was less bulky than the shotgun. He took it down and loaded it.

When he stood, the rifle's weight played havoc with the careful balance he'd just begun to learn that allowed him to favor his right leg. But he couldn't go out there without a weapon. He had no idea who was lurking in the shadow of the swamp, but he'd seen enough of a silhouette to know for a fact it was human, a two-legged rather than a four-legged predator.

Tristan set the alarm and carefully unlocked the French doors, making as little noise as possible. He chambered a round in the rifle and slipped out onto the patio. It was fortunate that the electricity was off. Otherwise the motion-detector lights on the patio and garage would come on, spotlighting him. When he reached the far corner of the garage, he stopped. His leg was aching badly and he was sweating in the rain-soaked air.

He stood with his back straight and solid against the exterior of the garage, as close as he could get to the corner without being seen. Then, carefully, keeping his gun at his side, he angled his head around and took a look at the area where he'd seen the shadow moving.

And there he was. Tristan took a quick mental picture of what he saw, then pulled back, flattening himself against the wall of the garage again. Staying alert to any sound, he ran the picture his brain had made. What all had he seen?

First, the shadow was not as tall as he'd initially thought. Could it be a kid, sneaking around, looking for alligators to poach?

He shook his head. No. The way the man stood upright, not crouched, the way he moved his upper body and the shape and size of his torso and head, told Tristan he was a full-grown man.

But what innocent reason would a man have to sneak around out here? The answer was, none. He had to be someone connected with the man who'd ordered Tristan's murder. But that man thought Tristan was dead. A horrible notion hit him.

As far as anyone knew, he *was* dead. So there was only one explanation for why the intruder was sneaking around. He was spying on Sandy.

Tristan glanced up at the sky, where clouds still hung low. He wished the moon would come out, but any light that illuminated the lurker's face would also illuminate his, so if the clouds parted, he needed to be ready for anything. He decided to take another look. When he angled his head around the corner of the building, his fears were realized.

The man held binoculars to his eyes. Even in the dark the vague shape of the man holding the binoculars and the direction he was looking were unmistakable. He was looking at the house. He was spying on Sandy.

The surprise morphed into anger, undercut by a gnawing fear. Who was he? Who had sent him?

Tristan picked up the rifle and took a deep breath. He had a lot to concentrate on. He had to aim the rifle, keep his balance, maintain his cool and keep an eagle eye on the other man.

He knew he was at a disadvantage, because he was to the man's left, so he'd have to step out into the open before he could even aim the rifle.

But when he peeked one more time, the lurker had lowered the binoculars and bent down. He was sneaking away.

After the man crawled for about a third of the way around the edge of the yard, he stood and ran toward the road. Tristan sneaked around the garage, hugging the wall, trying for one last glimpse of him.

He had reached the road now and was sprinting. In

the sky, the thunderclouds had begun to break up and a bit of pale moonlight shone through.

Tristan squinted. Even from this far away, as the man quickly ran toward the road, he looked familiar. He looked like Murray Cho.

"YOU HAVEN'T KEPT UP your end of the bargain," the voice said through the phone Murray held.

"But…I've done everything I can," Murray stammered. "It's not that easy. Have you ever tried to stalk someone?" The instant he heard himself say those words, he regretted them.

What the hell was he doing asking a question like that to someone who was ruthless enough to kidnap an innocent boy to coerce his father into spying on another innocent person?

The man could have stalked dozens of people and killed them for all Murray knew. His gruff, guttural voice certainly *sounded* cold and hard enough to be a killer's.

"Are you *kidding* me?" the man said with a harsh laugh. "You listen to me, Murray. My boss wants this information and he wants it fast! What's the big holdup?"

"I can't go around there in the daytime and it's hard to see anything at night. It's a new moon right now and—"

"I'm warning you, you little whiner—"

"Hold on," Murray said with much more bravado than he felt. "I'll not do anything until I find out if my son is alive—" He stopped because his voice broke. He cleared his throat. "Alive and well. I want to talk to him."

"You're skating on thin ice. There's only so much my boss will put up with and he's already had more than one problem this year. He's extremely nervous."

"I want to see my son. Kill me, but I won't do anything until I know he's alive."

"You can't see him until my boss sees what you've got," the man said harshly. "But I can let you hear his voice. Will that do?"

"Yes. Yes. Please."

Murray heard the other man cursing. Then he heard him calling loudly. "Get that punk in here." Pause. "You don't need to know why." More cursing. "Over here. Sit," he ordered.

Holding his breath, Murray listened for every sound. The man was obviously talking to his son. His heart squeezed in his chest until he thought it would burst from the pressure.

Then he heard his son's voice and a half sob caught in his throat. "Patrick!" he cried. "Patrick, are you all right?"

"Dad? What's going on? I don't get it—"

"All right, that's enough. Hey, you guys. Get him out of here."

"Dad! I think we're at—" Patrick's voice was cut off by an unmistakable sound. It was the sound of a fist hitting flesh.

"No!" Murray shouted. "Don't you touch my boy!"

"He's okay," the man said. "He just needs to learn to do what he's told and not try to be a smart-ass."

"He will. I promise he will."

"Listen to me. I don't need promises. I need action. Now, I'm going to give you a number to call and we'd better hear from you in forty-eight hours with the proof the boss needs, or neither you nor your son will see another sunset. Got it?"

Murray ached to tell the man what he wanted to know.

All he had to do was report that he'd seen a man with Mrs. DuChaud in her home through the binoculars, and he could get his son back safe and sound. He hoped.

But just as he opened his mouth he realized he'd be giving away everything with no promise of return. He couldn't prove to the kidnappers that the man with Mrs. DuChaud was Tristan DuChaud. He needed that proof as leverage.

"Yes. Got it," Murray said. With any luck he had the perfect way to ensure his son's safety. To get the proof he needed, he'd have to risk getting a lot closer to the house, and going in the daytime. That was not a problem. He'd do anything he had to in order to get a photo of Tristan DuChaud, because that was the only thing he could do to save his boy's life.

Chapter Six

The first thing Sandy noticed when she woke up the next morning was the smell of coffee. For a fleeting instant the dark aroma took her back to the days just after she'd found out she was pregnant, when Tristan was so excited about the baby. Knowing how much she loved coffee, he'd gone on a safari through South Louisiana looking for the absolute best decaf coffee in the state.

But on the heels of that poignant memory came harsh reality. This wasn't those early days. This was now.

Tristan was back from the dead and he'd spent the night in their house. She'd known he had because after she'd stormed out of the kitchen and down the hall to the master bedroom, she'd listened for the French doors to slam. They didn't.

She'd lain there for a few seconds, wondering if he'd left quietly. Then she heard the familiar, comforting beep of the alarm being armed. She'd gone right to sleep.

Sitting up and taking another whiff of the aroma of coffee sifting into the room, Sandy realized it had been five and a half months—her entire pregnancy so far—since she'd wanted a cup of coffee.

She turned on the lamp, but nothing happened. She'd forgotten the electricity was out. How had Tristan made coffee?

And what was the other aroma? Bacon? It must have been in the freezer. Maddy had put all the food that made Sandy nauseous into the freezer, and bacon had been a big culprit.

Right now, however, both the coffee and the bacon smelled heavenly. Sandy didn't care how Tristan had made them. She just hoped her nausea didn't come back as soon as she walked into the kitchen and got the full effects of the smells.

She jumped up, took a quick shower and dressed in a white skirt and pink top. The skirt had to go on top of her baby bump, so it came to just below her knees instead of just above her ankles, where it was supposed to be. But it looked fresh and new and maybe it would be a portent for the morning with Tristan.

When she stepped through the door into the kitchen, she understood how Tristan had cooked. He'd used the gas stove they kept in the laundry room for these circumstances. He'd used one burner to fry the bacon and had boiled water in a pan to make boiled coffee, sometimes known as hobo coffee.

He was at the kitchen table, sipping at a mug and playing with his food.

"What are you doing here?" she asked grumpily.

"Didn't you say you didn't care what I did, as long as you didn't have to look at me? I slept on the couch. I'll sleep outside tonight if you want me to."

"I *don't* want you to. I don't need you to protect me. You know how I know?" she asked. "I know because you left me alone for over two months. If you were so sure I needed protection, why didn't you come home? It's not like it was a long trip."

Tristan grimaced. "I couldn't."

She knew that. Of course he couldn't have, because he was in bed, at the very best too weak to stand, at worst, in a coma. She knew she'd have to ask Boudreau what had gone on during those weeks, because Tristan would never tell her.

"You went to a lot of trouble to find the gas stove and make breakfast. Why aren't you eating?"

He looked up at her and smiled, a tired smile that made her heart start to break. "I made it for you," he said. "You've lost weight and, at risk of sounding clichéd, you're eating for two."

"I've been nauseated at even the *thought* of bacon for months," she said, suppressing a smile. "And didn't you remember that all I could drink was grape juice?"

Tristan looked blank for a second, then his face turned a bright pink. He ducked his head. "Sorry," he said as he pushed his chair back from the table. "I'd forgotten that. I'll make you some toast."

"No." She put her hand on his arm. "Don't get up. The bacon and the coffee both smell good. I want to try them."

He looked down at her hand on his arm and, embarrassed, she pulled it away and sat down. She poured herself some coffee from the pot at her right hand, added a little sugar and stirred it. "Decaf?" she asked.

"Sure," he said, picking up a piece of bacon, then putting it down. He picked it up a second time and pressed it against the plate to break it. The bottom half shattered. "Bacon might be a little crisp," he said, sticking the half that was still intact into his mouth.

Sandy chuckled. "We never came to a compromise

about bacon, did we?" She picked up a piece and took a bite. "It *is* crispy," she said, making a face.

"That's what I just said."

She glanced up. He sounded irritated. "What's wrong?" she asked.

He shook his head and sighed.

"Don't sigh at me. What's wrong with you?"

He grabbed the wooden arms of the chair and shoved himself up out of the seat. "That's not the question," he barked. "The question is what's wrong with you? With *us*?" He pointed back and forth between them.

She watched him warily. She'd never seen him angry, not at her, and it sent a heart-thumping burst of adrenaline through her. An instant later, the baby stirred restlessly and she rubbed the side of her belly. "Are you saying—"

His gaze went to her hand and the look on his face made her heart hurt. "I'm saying I don't understand your attitude. I thought you'd at least be happy to see me."

Sandy gave him a shocked look. "Happy? I suppose you mean because you were so thrilled to see me and you came all this way. In case you don't remember, when I saw you, you were trying to sneak in and out of here without me catching you. Name one thing—just one— about it that should make me *happy*?"

He leveled his gaze on her in a game of visual chicken. "Maybe the fact that I wasn't dead?" he said softly.

She couldn't hold his gaze. Of course he was right. She *had* been stunned and thrilled that he was alive, after she'd recovered from the initial shock. Then she'd woken up thinking she was having another hallucination. There had been no room inside her for happiness.

"When I first saw you—" She held up a hand. "No. I'm not going to go into all that again. Tristan, you know how I feel. If you can't accept that I have a right to be angry, then…well, I don't know what else I can tell you."

He didn't like her answer. There was no mistaking that. A muscle in his lean jaw ticked and at his temple, a vein stood out in sharp relief. "Oh, great," he said, his voice heavy with irony. "That explains everything."

She opened her mouth to spit out a sharp retort, but he kept talking.

"I'm headed over to Boudreau's," he said through gritted teeth, "but first I'm going to take a look around the area where I saw Murray last night. Now that the sun's up, I might be able to find a clue as to what he was doing here this time."

"Whoa! What?" Sandy gasped. "You saw Murray? Are you talking about Murray Cho?"

Tristan muttered a curse under his breath. He obviously had not meant to say that out loud. He opened his mouth, then closed it, then opened it again.

"Damn it, Tristan. Stop trying to not tell me anything. I need to know what's going on so I can take care of myself."

"Fine. Yes, it was Murray Cho. He was sneaking around in the weeds on the other side of the garage."

"Murray? But he's in Gulfport. He moved."

"All I can say is I saw him and recognized him. I can't tell you why he was here. That's why I'm going to check," he said with exaggerated patience.

She crossed her arms, a little creeped out. "I saw Murray's son peeking in the master bedroom window on the day of your funeral. Murray was behind him."

"What were they doing?"

Sandy shook her head. "I assumed Patrick had wandered around the house and was peeking in to see what he could see. Murray followed him to stop him." She paused. "How are you so sure this was Murray?"

"I saw his face when the moon came out for a few seconds."

"What do you think he was doing here?" she said. "Do you know he was involved in bringing down the smugglers?"

Tristan nodded. "Yeah. Boudreau told me he showed up at the seafood warehouse threatening to take them all down."

"Did Boudreau tell you he shot first? Boudreau killed the oil rig captain without blinking an eye." She sent him a sidelong glance. "Maddy told me Boudreau said, 'This is for Tristan,' or something like that."

Tristan's brows shot up. "No. He never mentioned that, but I suppose he wouldn't." He was quiet for a moment.

"There's something else about Murray, isn't there? You said 'this time.'"

He looked down at his hands and back up at her. "Did I?"

She set her jaw and stared at him. "Don't be coy. You said, 'What he was doing here this time.'"

"Have you got your laptop?" he asked.

"No. As a matter of fact, somebody stole it from the nursery. It was gone when I got back here." The look on his face unnerved her. "Why?"

"Boudreau was checking on the house a couple of weeks ago and he saw Murray coming out the French doors with what looked like your laptop."

"And he's sure it was Murray. A hundred percent sure?"

"What is it with you and Murray?"

"Nothing," Sandy said. "I felt bad that he thought he

had to leave Bonne Chance after the incident with the smugglers at his seafood warehouse. He always seemed so nice and quiet. But this makes the third time he's been sneaking around. What do you think he's looking for?"

"He's watching you."

That surprised her. "Me? Why? Are you sure?"

"Oh, I'm sure."

Sandy stared at him. His tone had been almost amused. "I don't get it. How can you be?"

"Because you were here in the kitchen and he was directly across the yard, in that patch of weeds, with binoculars."

Sandy looked in the direction Tristan pointed. It had been frightening to see Patrick Cho and his father standing at her bedroom window on the day of Tristan's funeral. But as she pictured Murray lurking out there in the dark and watching her through binoculars, she felt sick.

She turned back to Tristan, but he was gone. She hadn't heard him open the door. She stepped out onto the patio and looked in the direction of the dock, but he'd already disappeared into the heavy canopy of branches, weeds and vines that hid the path from casual view. He'd gone back to Boudreau's cabin.

She went inside, her fury at him rising with every breath she took. How dare he act so supercilious? He wasn't the only person who'd been hurt. She'd nearly died of grief and unbearable loss when she found out he was dead. The only thing that had kept her alive during those first hours and days was the knowledge that if she took her life, she'd be taking another innocent life with her.

She hadn't been able to even think about doing that to her baby. Instead, she'd vowed to make sure her child lacked for nothing and knew everything she could possibly tell him…or her…about his father.

"I swear, little bean, sometimes I don't know why I bother. What's the matter with him? Staying away for my safety. What a jerk. If everyone thinks he's dead, how could he possibly draw the bad guys to me?" She stopped. "Unless— Oh, dear God."

She sat down and cradled her tummy in her hands. "That's what's bothering Tristan—your daddy," she said. "Murray Cho is working for…for whoever tried to kill him. He must have been sent by them to watch me, to see if I acted strangely. He must be trying to find out if Tristan is really dead. Because if Tristan is alive, he could ruin them—maybe even put them in prison.

"What if Murray saw him, bean?"

BY LATE AFTERNOON, Sandy was climbing the walls. She'd tried to distract herself by taking inventory of their stock of food and planning what to cook, but that only kept her occupied for about a half hour.

So she decided to practice her crochet. She'd taken a class and now she was knitting the bean a pair of booties, but they were looking a little more like gloves than booties. Her stitches stuck out here and there.

Finally, she tossed the crocheting aside and stood and looked out the French doors toward the path to the dock, but nothing was stirring. Maybe Tristan had decided he needed some peace and quiet, so he was planning to stay at Boudreau's.

It had been around five hours or so since he'd left. Under normal circumstances he occasionally spent all afternoon and sometimes all evening with his Cajun friend, talking and fishing or just drinking beer.

But these weren't normal circumstances and Sandy wanted to talk to her husband.

She flung the French doors open and stepped out onto the patio. "You're not going to leave me here all day and night by myself, Tristan DuChaud. Not now that I know you're alive, you lying liar." She patted the side of her belly where the bean was beginning to kick.

"Hey, bean, it's okay. Don't worry. I'm not really *that* mad at your daddy. It's just that he's the stubbornest, most arrogant man in three counties." The baby kicked her again.

"Okay, okay," she whispered. "I'm through being mad. We're going to go over to Boudreau's place and find your daddy. And when we do, I'm playing the alone-and-scared card. Because if there's one thing you need to remember, it's that your daddy might be stubborn, but your mama is downright obstinate." She chuckled. "With us for parents, you're going to be a piece of work, aren't you?"

She walked briskly across the yard to the overgrown path. Before she stepped into the tangle of weeds and vines, she glanced toward the place where Tristan had said that Murray Cho had been hiding and watching her. *Through binoculars.* She drew her shoulders up as a frisson of aversion slithered down her spine.

She stood still for a moment and closed her eyes. Did she feel someone's eyes on her? She didn't think so. But would she, even if there were someone watching her? She had no idea.

Just as she put out a hand to brush away hanging vines so she could step onto the path, she heard something—footsteps—coming her way. Maybe it was Tristan. Her heart fluttered a little bit.

But what if it was Murray? Suddenly frightened, she turned to run back across the yard, but the person who'd been trampling down the path ran slap into her, grunting at the impact.

"Tristan!" she cried as he stumbled against her, trying not to lose his footing on the slippery leaves and sticky vines on the ground. She heard a muffled thump as his walking stick hit the ground.

"Sandy! What are you doing out here? Where do you think you're going?"

"To find you. You've been gone for hours," she complained.

"Well, you told me to leave, and in no uncertain terms, either."

"I did not," she shot back, but then she remembered. She'd said, *Leave. Just leave.*

"I didn't mean for you to stay gone. I was afraid you weren't coming back. It hurt so much I wanted to die when I found out you were dead. Staying away, letting me think you were dead, just might be the worst thing any man has ever done to his wife."

He shook his head. "I think that's a bit of an exaggeration," he said in that reasonable, mockingly patient tone that always made her furious. And right now was no different.

"Oh!" she shrieked, doubling her hands into fists. "I swear you make me so mad, I could—I could—"

"What, Sandy?" Tristan asked, stepping toward her, his pale face drawn, his eyes dark and deep as brown bottle glass in the sun. He was in her face and she couldn't look away.

"That's just it. I don't know. What I'd like to do is reach into your heart and pull out the man I married. Because you're not him. You think you haven't changed? Well, you're wrong. You've changed, a lot."

Tristan's jaw tensed.

"And I'm not talking about just since you went overboard. No. It's been going on for a long time now. A year, at least." She stopped, calculating in her head. "Oh, my God, that's it, isn't it? You became a Homeland Security agent a year ago." She stopped, but he didn't say anything. "Isn't it?" she cried.

Tristan's face hadn't changed, but his dark brown eyes seemed to get even darker. "Yes," he said.

She didn't want to look at him. She'd told him the truth. He was not the person she'd known all her life, not the person she'd married. She turned away. "I don't know who you are anymore."

She felt his gaze burning into her back, but he didn't say a word.

"I think Murray is working for the man who tried to have you killed," she said.

For a couple of seconds, Tristan stayed quiet. Finally he said, "I do, too."

"You do?" She stared at him. "What are you going to do? We've got to stop him!"

"That's what Boudreau and I have been talking about."

"Tell me something. If you're so worried about me, why are we still here? Why haven't we gone somewhere else—somewhere safe, where I can have my baby without having to worry that his father is going to be dead before he's born?" She took a deep breath.

"And while you're explaining things, what are we supposed to do without you? What is your child supposed to do?" Anger flared inside her and constricted her throat. She struggled to take a full breath. "I'll promise you this, Tristan Francois DuChaud," she continued, walking up to him and jabbing her forefinger into the middle of his chest. "I will protect this baby with all my power. I'll risk *anything*," she said. "My life—even yours—for this baby's life."

Tristan grabbed her by the upper arms and pulled her so close that his face was a mere fraction of an inch from hers.

"You don't think I would do the same thing?" he said through clenched teeth. After all this time—after a lifetime together—are you telling me you don't know that? You don't know that I would die for you or for our baby? But I don't intend for it to come to that. Boudreau and I are working on a plan to keep you and the baby safe until we can figure out who is behind all this and how to get to him."

"Stop it," Sandy cried. She'd never had the full effect of Tristan's blazing eyes boring into hers in anger. "Let go. You're scaring me."

He let go instantly—so fast that Sandy had to catch herself to keep from losing her balance. The anger drained from his face. "Sorry. I didn't mean to do that."

"That's just it, Tristan. You didn't mean to scare me. You didn't mean to make me think you were dead. You didn't *mean to do* a lot of things. But you have. And I know it's because of that stupid job. Why would you do that? Why on earth would you become an undercover agent? That's not you."

He looked at her for a moment, then turned toward the house. "Go inside and go to bed. You need some sleep. I'll lock up the house and put the alarm on."

"No. I want an answer."

But she didn't get one. Tristan started walking in his

awkward way toward the house. She had no choice but to follow him or stand outside alone. Inside, he set the alarm and asked her if she wanted coffee.

She shook her head.

"Yeah, me neither," he said. He walked down the hall into the master bedroom.

Sandy didn't know what to say, so she followed him. Finally, he spoke.

"I never wanted to work on the oil rigs," he said. "I saw my dad turn hard and distant. He was out there more than he was home. I hated that and I swore I would never do that to my—" He stopped.

"To your family," Sandy supplied, hearing the bitter note in her voice.

"But I had no choice."

"Are you blaming me?"

He shook his head. "No, of course not. I'm not blaming anyone. Dad died and I had to forget about veterinary school and get a job. The oil rigs have always paid the best.

"It happened. Nobody's fault. But when Homeland Security contacted me and told me they wanted an agent on the *Pleiades Seagull* who was a local and would never be suspected of being undercover for the government, it sounded like a way of making the job meaningful. I wouldn't just be one man on one of the thousands of oil rigs in the Gulf of Mexico—I'd be doing something for my country." He shrugged.

Sandy's heart wrenched, listening to his dreams. She took a step toward him, reached out and put her hand on his shoulder. "I guess I never realized how much it meant to you to be able to contribute to the safety and security of the country."

His back stiffened. "I'll sleep on the sofa in the living room," he said flatly. "That way I can see and hear anyone who might be sneaking around the house. We'll have the alarm, but I'd like to get a look at whoever it is that's hanging around. If I do see someone, I might set off the alarm myself just to be able to get to him and beat the crap out of him."

She scowled at him. "Don't even try," she said with more than a dash of sarcasm. "You couldn't beat the crap out of a stuffed toy bear in the condition you're in."

Chapter Seven

As soon as the words were out of her mouth, Sandy was sorry. Tristan's face went still and his mouth flattened.

"You've always underestimated me, San. I'm not sure why."

"I'm not underestimating you. I'm looking at you. You're injured. You don't have your strength back. Of course you can't fight until you're healed. But you're not by nature a fighter, anyhow. You're a romantic. A peacekeeper." She held up a hand when Tristan started to speak.

"I know. I know you can take care of yourself—and me. I've never doubted that. But you've never been the type to go looking for trouble."

He shook his head. "That's not what I'm doing. I'm talking about protecting my house. Protecting you and the baby. But there you go, underestimating me again." He looked down then back up at her. "I'll see you in the morning."

"Tristan?" she called out just as he was about to close the door behind him.

He looked at her. "Yeah?"

"Don't go."

"I thought you were so mad at me you could do something drastic."

"I am— I was."

"So what were you thinking of?" he asked, his mood lightening. His mouth turned up in a mischievous smile. "This?" And he drew her to him and kissed her.

Sandy was completely caught off guard. She wouldn't have been surprised if he'd shaken her or pushed her out of the way and strode out of the house. But kiss her? That, she'd never suspected.

All those thoughts flitted through her head in a split second. Practically no time. Yet time enough for him to begin to nibble at her lips and flick them with his tongue in a tentative invitation for her to open her mouth.

She had no problem complying with that request. Nothing about this part of their life together had changed at all. She was still in love with her husband, still turned on by the faintest pressure of his lips on hers, the quickest, lightest nibble on the flesh of her lips and tongue and every breathtaking inch that his hands caressed as they moved from her back around to the sides of her breasts.

She moaned and opened her mouth, using her tongue the way he was using his, to thrust and explore and ease her way closer and closer. She felt faint with desire, a sensation she'd known—*known*—she would never feel again, because the man she'd loved ever since they were children was dead. And if it hadn't been for his child who was growing within her, her heart would have died, too.

From long before they'd experimented with something more than kissing or innocent hand holding or hugging, she'd been insatiably drawn to him. She'd wanted him touching her, molding his body to hers, loving her, all the time. They'd both been seventeen, too young and yet plenty old enough.

Still, once they'd done *it*, there was no turning back. They had loved each other all their lives. And that love had always been multifaceted. It embodied every kind of love in existence: sexual, sensual, platonic, innocent and jaded all at once. They were not perfect people, by any means, but they were perfect together.

As the fuel of desire flowed through Sandy, her longing for the man she had and would always love and whom she'd thought she'd lost forever grew until she was on the verge of bursting into climactic flame just from his mouth on hers and his hands caressing her.

"This is probably not a good idea," he murmured against her lips.

"You started it," she teased, but she felt the change in him. He was withdrawing. She didn't know what his problem was, but she wasn't about to give up so easily.

She had always wanted him, but at this moment, her desire for him was a burning urge like nothing she'd ever felt before. He'd been dead and now he was alive, his skin vibrant and hot, his body coursing with life. She slid her arms around his waist and kept kissing him.

For an instant he yielded. He deepened his kiss, sending electric pulses through her, each one bringing her closer and closer to the brink of climax. She pressed her body against his.

"No," he said. He stiffened and pulled away.

Sandy moaned. "Don't stop now," she whispered.

"San," he said, putting his hands on her upper arms and holding her at arm's length. He met her gaze, then he looked away. "I'm not sure I can…do this," he muttered.

She looked up at him with a small smile. "I'm sure

you can," she said, sliding her fingers across the front of his pants.

He stepped away from her and turned his back. "That's not what I'm talking about."

"Then what?" she asked.

He said something, too softly for her to understand.

She went to him and tried to wrap her arms around him from behind, but he pulled away and turned, his face dark with anger.

"Damn it, Sandy, I can barely walk. My damn leg will never hold up to—" He gestured vaguely.

Sandy gave a short laugh. "You don't have to. I can definitely handle that workload myself. I'll be on top and—"

"I said no!" he snapped, looking cornered.

Sandy held up her hands, palms out. She took a step backward. "Fine. Sorry," she said. Her whole body ached with the pain of thwarted desire as well as hurt at his rejection.

He shot her a glare, then said, "Okay, well, I'm going to lie down on the couch."

She closed her eyes and then opened them again. "I'd feel a lot better if you'd stay in my—our—room," she said. "If you want, you can sleep on the daybed."

Tristan looked at the small bed then back at her. "Nope. I'm not sleeping on some child-sized bed in my own bedroom in my own house. You can forget that. If you want me to stay in this room—our room—it will be in my bed with my wife."

At his words, the flame inside her that he'd so successfully damped just a few seconds ago reignited.

It was a flame that had been banked for a long time. Too long. It had been a long time since she'd been in the same bed with her husband. Before he'd fallen or been pushed overboard, he'd been on the rig for a month. The last time he'd come home she'd been dealing with a severe bout of morning sickness. Amazed, she realized it had been over four months since they had made love.

"Good night," Tristan said, heading out the door again. "Get some sleep."

"Wait!" she cried.

He stopped and stood in the doorway, rubbing his temple with his fingers.

She looked at him. He was a miracle by anyone's account. He'd been declared dead. He'd had funeral rites spoken over a casket that supposedly contained his remains. Now he had returned. And she needed him as close to her as was humanly possible. "All right," she said.

"All right what?" he asked, earning a glare from her. "Just so we're clear."

"Please sleep in here with me, in the bed," she said. "I need you with me."

He nodded slowly, his dark eyes shimmering like gems in the low light.

IT WAS A long time before Tristan came to bed. Sandy didn't know exactly what time he'd slipped beneath the covers, but when she awoke at 2:00 a.m., her heart pounding and her breath puffing in shallow gasps, he was there.

He'd put his hand on her arm and bent his head to her ear. "Go back to sleep, *cher.* I'm here now."

"Tristan?" she whispered, turning over and snuggling into his arms. "I heard something."

She felt him stiffen slightly and couldn't tell if it was because she'd turned a casual gesture of comfort into an embrace or because of what she'd said.

"I know," he said. "It's probably the wind."

"Probably? You think it might be something to worry about?" She snuggled closer.

His breath caught. "San, be careful."

"Oh, Tristan, did I hurt you? I'm sorry," she said.

"No, but you're going to wake us up if you don't stop talking."

She pressed her nose into the side of his neck. He smelled the same as he always had. Warm, clean, masculine. She'd never quite figured out what the combination of scents was. Something like soap and shaving cream and maybe a little toothpaste, mingled with a masculine undertone that was uniquely his. To her, he smelled like the man she'd sworn to live the rest of her life with.

"Are you sure you want me to be careful?" she whispered into his ear.

He shivered and she felt goose bumps raise on the sensitive skin beneath his ear. She blew on it, hoping to keep the goose bumps there for as long as possible.

"Is that careful enough?" she whispered. She shouldn't be trying to seduce him. She knew that. For one thing, she was still angry with him for not letting her know that he was alive for two whole months. Granted, he'd spent most of one of those months either unconscious or asleep, recuperating on any day of those two months. But Boudreau could have walked over and saved her hours and days of horrible grief and sadness. He could have told her that Tristan was alive.

But even more than anger, she was feeling a deep, exquisitely painful yearning for him. He was her husband and it had been way too long since they'd made love.

"What are you doing?" he asked, his voice breathy and deep.

"I'm doing what I thought you wanted me to do," she said, thinking she was treading on dangerous ground. If he chose to get annoyed with her for bringing that up, she'd lose her chance to make love with her husband.

Tristan rose up on his elbow and looked down at her. "And what's that, *cher*?" he whispered.

She smiled up at him, knowing from the tone of his voice and the soft look in his dark eyes that he'd made his decision. He was ready to be her husband, her living, breathing, virile husband.

"Welcoming you home," she breathed, barely even making a sound. But she knew he heard it and understood it. He pulled her into his arms and kissed her with as much intensity, as much desire, as much love as he ever had.

Sandy melted into his embrace and took his kiss, fully, returning it the same way. When he touched and caressed her, when he kissed her, she felt like an ethereal, exquisite fairy, floating in a beautiful world that belonged to just the two of them, her and Tristan. Three, now that the little bean was with them.

Tristan slid a hand down over her rounded belly. "Hi, bean," he whispered. Then he bent his head and kissed the taut skin. "Hey, my little boy. My son. How're you doing in there?"

Sandy felt his hand travel down the slope of the baby bump and farther, to caress her intimately. When his fingers touched her, a painfully thrilling spasm shot through her with the speed and sense of an electric shock. She cried out.

Immediately, he tried to pull his hand away, but she held it there with hers. "Don't stop, please. It's been so long."

"I know," he gasped. "I didn't mean to leave you alone so long." He bent to lick and nibble on her distended nipples as his arousal hardened against her thigh.

Sandy arched her back, the twin sensations of his mouth on her nipples and his fingers inside her driving her to a second climax, stronger than the first. While she was still receiving little aftershocks of that second climax, Tristan suckled on a nipple.

"Tris, just so you know, I'm getting some—"

He jerked backward so quickly that, even though she was in the middle of explaining what he might encounter, it shocked Sandy.

"What? Did you hear something?" she asked, but she was pretty sure he wasn't fixated on anything that had happened outside.

He was wiping his mouth and staring at her breast. "Was that—" he asked, looking pale.

She nodded and smiled. "Milk. Just a little bit. I've been noticing little droplets every so often."

"I'm not sure I want to know that," he muttered.

She was still shaky from her climaxes, so when she reached out for him, her hand trembled. "It's fine, Tris. It's perfectly natural. In fact, some couples do this. It stimulates the production of the milk and makes it easier for—"

"Okay," he snapped, swiping a hand through the air. "Could you just stop?" He pulled away from her and got up. "I'm going to sleep on the couch, like I said I would in the first place," he said more calmly. "I need some sleep and I'm sure you do, too."

He stood, steadying himself against the bedpost as he retrieved his jeans from a chair. As he headed out the door, she saw his silhouette in briefs and a T-shirt. His right lower leg appeared to be nothing but skin and bone.

He closed the door behind him and Sandy flopped down on the bed, staring at the ceiling. She needed a few seconds to recover from the two—had it just been two?—climaxes.

The feeling of Tristan touching her, caressing her, dipping into her, was so sharp and sweetly painful that she wanted to capture as much of it as she could before the last of the tiny aftershocks faded.

She also wanted to get up and follow Tristan and force him with kisses and touches to finish what he'd started. It was late, though, and he'd been shocked and repulsed when he'd tasted the milk from her breast. He hadn't been ready for that.

A deep pain arrowed through her entire body. Maybe he would never be ready for it, or for her, again, after the horror he'd been through. She couldn't imagine the pain and fear he'd suffered, certain he would die, or if he lived that he would be scarred and, worse, never have full use of his leg again.

For the first time it occurred to her that she may have had it easier than he had. It was beyond awful to find out the love of your life was dead, but was it worse than experiencing death? Especially a violent death? Was it worse than watching a vicious creature rip away a part of your body? Was it worse than needing air and sucking in seawater instead?

Tears slipped down her cheeks and wet her face and her pillow she allowed herself to think about what it had been like for him. Dear God, how she loved him. And how she had let him down.

WHEN SHE WOKE just after eight o'clock, Tristan was in bed with her. She was lying on her side and his body was spooning hers. His half-hard arousal was pressed against her and his deep, even breaths tickled her ear. But what sent a poignant ache through her was that his hand was resting protectively on her tummy. She wanted to turn and lay her hands over his, wanted to show him the heart-filling thrill of feeling his baby kick and squirm inside her. She longed to lie there in his arms and tell him how the doctor had joked about that little thing he saw on the sonogram that made him sure the baby was a boy.

She listened to Tristan's soft, even breaths and felt the supple firmness of his arm embracing her. He was sleeping soundly. From the shadows beneath his eyes, she knew it had been a long time since he'd slept well, so she didn't want to disturb him.

She dozed for another hour before her own restlessness forced her to slide quietly out of bed, doing her best not to wake him.

As she poured a glass of juice, she glanced at the calendar. It was still on April. She took it off the wall and turned it to June. She'd spent almost two months in a grief-stricken haze, staying with her mother-in-law. Then last week she'd decided to come home. She'd gotten here Sunday. Her finger slid across the calendar page. And today was Friday.

Her mind reeled, thinking about all that had happened in just five days.

She hung the calendar back up and made a pot of hobo coffee on the gas stove, then wiped stray grounds off the counter.

Five days and she'd gone from widow back to wife—abandoned wife.

Throughout their entire lives, through good times and bad, she'd always believed she could count on Tristan's love to overcome any and all obstacles. His love had always been so steady, always there as a foundation that their relationship rested on, no matter what.

But now he'd done the one thing that just might crumble their marriage. From the time they were nine years old, he'd been by her side.

Then, within a heartbeat, he was gone.

The hilarious irony was that he hadn't died after all—he'd abandoned her. He'd left her alone and carrying his child. She folded the dishrag and laid it on the edge of the sink, then she rubbed her baby bump.

"I don't know if we can survive this, little bean." She blinked away tears and took a deep breath, ordering herself not to cry. "We'll try, I know. For your sake. And more than anything, I want to protect you. Because if your daddy could let me think he was dead, how can I risk that he might do something similar to you?"

The idea of her little boy looking for their father and finding him gone ate a hole the size of a shark bite into Sandy's heart. She could not—she *would not*—allow that to happen to her child. Not even if she had to give up love.

At that instant something large and heavy crashed into the French doors, sending Sandy stumbling backward in an instinctive fight-or-flight response.

The doors hadn't broken as she'd instantly thought, but all she could see was a bizarrely flattened face and hands pressed against the door. She half screamed. Her chest contracted and her scalp burned with fear. She took another step backward and another, until her back hit the refrigerator.

"Tris—" she started, but her voice fell flat. There wasn't enough air from her paralyzed lungs to make a sound. She struggled just to breathe. Her arms and legs were limp.

Forcing herself to reach for one of the knives in the block on the counter, she tried to wrap her fingers around its handle, but they weren't working right, which was probably just as well. What she thought she would do with the knife if she could grab it, she had no idea.

She sucked in air again, this time managing to get a full breath. "Tristan," she cried, dismayed at her tentative, breathy tone.

She was still staring at the misshapen face when suddenly it jerked backward and she could make out features. She almost fainted in surprise and fear. It was Murray Cho.

"No!" she cried. "Tristan!" She felt behind her as she sidled toward the edge of the refrigerator so she could make a beeline for the hall.

To her surprise, Murray didn't move. He didn't try to break down the doors or run. He appeared to be paralyzed, or frozen with fear himself. His dark, almond-shaped eyes pleaded with her, for what, she didn't know.

He looked as scared, if not more, than she felt. Then within a heartbeat, he flew backward as if pulled by a bungee cord and his expression changed to surprise, then pure terror.

Before she could wonder what had happened, she saw something behind him move. Her brain was still having trouble reconciling what she saw with reality, because the reality was that Murray looked as if he were being jerked around by a puppet master.

She kept inching toward the door.

"Tristan!" she yelled, and this time her voice worked. She was just about to duck around the door facing into the hall and shove it closed when she caught a glimpse of another face, this one dark and familiar. It was Boudreau. His dark gaze met hers.

"Tris-tan!" she shrieked.

He burst into the kitchen as Boudreau reached for the door handle.

"San? Are you all right?" he cried, stopping cold when he saw Boudreau.

"Hold it!" Tristan called out and backtracked into the hall to turn off the alarm. Then he opened the French doors. "Boudreau," Tristan greeted the older man.

"Tristan," Boudreau replied.

"What have you got here?" Tristan said as if he were looking at a gift bag in Boudreau's hand, rather than a man at the end of his gun barrel.

"Me, I'm thinking I caught me a poacher, yeah," Boudreau said. "Found him wandering around here early this morning. I spent some time talking to him, but he don't want to talk to me. So me, I brought him to you."

Sandy gasped and looked at Murray. She'd always thought he was a nice, quiet man, even after the incident at her bedroom window.

But Boudreau had seen him leaving her house with her laptop, and Tristan had seen him spying on them with binoculars.

Right now, he looked terrified. She frowned, trying to reconcile the pleasant fisherman with a man who was essentially stalking her.

Boudreau described exactly how he'd gotten the drop on Murray. "Was he armed?" Tristan asked.

"*Oui*, in a manner of speaking," Boudreau said. He pulled a smartphone and a small pair of binoculars out of his pocket. "Not dangerous weapons, unless they get into the wrong hands."

"What's going on here, Murray? I saw you the other night, sneaking around the side of my garage with those binoculars. I know you took my wife's laptop."

"Mr. DuChaud, please," Murray Cho said. "Can I talk to you? I try to explain to Mr. Boudreau, but he won't listen."

Sandy noticed that Murray's English was deteriorating. Could fear do that? Because he was obviously afraid. He was sweating profusely and looked as if he were being led to the hangman's noose. His eyes were sunken, as were his cheeks.

"Please, Mr. DuChaud," he begged.

"Tristan?" Sandy called, wanting to tell him to not be too hard on him. But Tristan waved a hand at her dismissively.

That made her angry. She walked closer to the doors, her arms crossed, intent on hearing every scrap of conversation. Tristan glanced toward her, frowning, but she ignored him.

"Where was he?" he asked Boudreau.

"Right back there," Boudreau said, pointing to the other side of the garage. "He looked like he was waiting to sneak up to the house and grab some pictures."

"Murray," Sandy said quickly. "What's going on? Why were you spying on us?"

Murray turned his gaze to her, hope flaring like a tiny candle flame in a storm.

"Sandy," Tristan said warningly.

"He's terrified," she shot back at him. "Can't you see that?"

"He oughtta be. I got my double-barrel pointed right at his heart," Boudreau responded.

"You don't think this is more than just fear of being caught?" She stepped closer. "Murray? I know the day of the funeral you were just trying to stop Patrick from looking in my window. I understand that. Your son is what—barely eighteen? But you're afraid of more than that, aren't you? What is it, Murray? You can tell us."

"Damn it, Sandy," Tristan snapped, taking her arm and pulling her back. "Don't get so close to him. We don't know what he might do."

Murray's head started going back and forth, back and forth in a negative response. "No, no, no. I won't hurt you, Mrs. DuChaud. Not you. I'm so sorry. So sorry."

"Murray, calm down," Sandy continued. "Why don't you tell me what's wrong."

She felt Tristan's glare. "Stop it, San. He's not a hurt dog or an abandoned kitten. Go back into the bedroom and let us handle this."

Who was this man who had come back to her? It wasn't her Tristan. Tristan had never treated her as anything less than equal in their lives. She propped her fists on her hips.

"I will not be sent off to the bedroom like a child. And you could at least untie him," Sandy pushed back at him. "He may not be a puppy or a kitten, but he's not a wild boar, either. But that's how Boudreau has him trussed, as if he's ready for the spit."

Boudreau spoke up. "I watched for him and got him, like you wanted me to, Tristan. But me, I ain't no bounty hunter, and anyhow, this man got no bounty on him. So what you want me to do with him?"

"Murray?" Tristan sighed and turned back to Cho. "Will you talk to me? Tell me what's going on here? And not try anything?"

"Oh, yes, sir," Murray said. "Sure. Sure, I talk."

Tristan nodded to Boudreau, who opened his shotgun and emptied the shells from the barrels, then closed it again, leaving it ready to be cocked if necessary. He set it against the door facing and, with a single snap of his wrist, untied Murray's hands.

In a flash, Murray shoved Boudreau aside and took off as fast as he could, considering Boudreau had hobbled him with rope.

Tristan started after him immediately, but he knew he was doomed to failure. Even hobbled, the fisherman had a distinct advantage over Tristan with his bad leg. Still, Tristan did his best, feeling the excruciating pain in his right leg with every step.

But while Murray was faster, his short legs weren't made for the irregular terrain. He tripped on a mound of dirt that covered a mole tunnel and went down. Tristan stopped, gulping in lungfuls of air, straining for oxygen. Boudreau walked past him and yanked Murray up by the collar. "You try that again, you, and I'll treat you to a butt full of bird shot, *n'est-ce pas*?"

Murray nodded furiously.

Tristan straightened, but he was still gasping for breath. "Take him back to…the house, Boudreau, and tie his hands again," he said haltingly.

"You got no business running, you," Boudreau said to Tristan. "You'll undo all the good we done."

Tristan didn't answer. He just glared at Boudreau for

saying that in front of Murray Cho, because he was now absolutely sure that Murray worked for his enemy.

"Let's go," Boudreau said, jerking Murray in the direction of the house. "March."

Tristan followed at a healthy distance, favoring his leg until he finally caught his breath. He'd never been in such rotten condition in his entire life. Not even the summer he suffered a collapsed lung in a touch football game that turned into a brawl. He was furious with his weakness and terrified that this was the best he was ever going to be.

No! He stopped those thoughts. He *would* get back his strength and agility. He'd do whatever he had to do to be the man he'd been before. But until then, he had to face the truth. He had no way to protect Sandy and their baby except by using his brain, and against enemies with lethal—probably automatic—weapons, his brain, as good as it was, would not be enough.

Chapter Eight

When Tristan limped back into the kitchen, Murray was seated at the table and Boudreau was standing near the French doors with his shotgun pointed at the fisherman. Sandy had just set a glass of cold water in front of Murray and was talking to Boudreau.

"Could you please put the shotgun down?" she asked.

Boudreau shook his head. "No, ma'am, Miss Sandy. And no," he said when she opened her mouth again, "I don't want any water. Ain't changed my mind from ten seconds ago," Boudreau grumbled.

Sandy shot the Cajun an irritated look, then turned the same look on Tristan. When she met his gaze, she frowned.

"I could use some cold water," he said.

"I'm sure you could," she snapped. "Why would you take off running like that? After everything you've been through, and with that leg not even healed yet? What are you trying to do? Kill yourself?"

Tristan felt a hot rage building up inside him, fueled by pain, exhaustion and humiliation. He clenched his jaw, trying to keep from firing a nasty response back at her. He told himself she was worried about him, but he had the sinking feeling this was how it was going to be from now on. Him fighting a losing battle to regain her respect and prove to her that he was not less of a man because of his injury, and her treating him like a fragile invalid.

It occurred to him that he'd stayed with Boudreau longer than absolutely necessary in an effort to hide from this reality, this truth that he would never be the man he'd been before.

Sandy's expression softened. "Sorry. I shouldn't have said that."

Tristan's face felt hot. *Stop. You're making it worse.* Aloud he said, "Never mind that. Can you get me some water?" he asked again.

He knew by her expression that even though she apologized, this was not the end of it. He was going to get an earful once they were alone. He rubbed his forehead and considered trading places with Boudreau. He'd guard Murray and let Boudreau deal with Sandy. But even as the thought entered his head he almost had to smile. Boudreau had more sense than to fall for a deal like that.

And he was wasting time, He needed to find out everything Murray Cho knew and he needed to do it now. He sat down opposite Murray. "Sit if you want, Boudreau."

The Cajun shook his head. "What I want is to get back to the house and check on that pig roast I put on this morning, but I can't do that till you decide what you going to do about this." He angled his head in the general direction of Murray Cho.

"Murray, you know me, right?"

"Yes, sir, Mr. DuChaud. Yes, sir." Murray's command of English was almost back to normal now that he'd calmed down. "I'm glad you're not dead."

"I let you use the DuChaud dock sometimes, right?"

"All the time, Mr. DuChaud. I appreciate it."

"So why were you sneaking around on my land spying on my wife?"

The Vietnamese fisherman's face turned a sickly pale yellow color. "I can't say, Mr. DuChaud. I can't. I can't."

"You don't have to be afraid of me or Boudreau. Just tell us why you're lurking around and who put you up to it and we'll leave you completely alone."

"No, no, no. That will not work. I can't tell you. It will be awful. No, please no. Just let me go. Please."

Sandy was right. The man was terrified of someone, but it wasn't Boudreau and it sure wasn't him.

"And let you get close enough to my wife to hurt her or kill her? Hell no."

Murray shook his head, looking disappointed in Tristan. "Mrs. DuChaud should go away. Take her away for a long time. Then she be safe."

Tristan vaulted up and slapped his palms down on the table. "That's it. *That's it!* I'm not waiting any longer for answers, Murray. I'll put you in the car and we'll go to the sheriff's office right now and you'll be locked up until you decide to tell me what I want to know."

He'd banked on Murray not wanting to go to jail, on him being so scared that he'd blurt out the information he needed, but there was someone who frightened Murray more than Tristan.

"More than me," he said, then realized he'd spoken aloud. "You're scared to death, aren't you?" he asked Murray.

Murray shook his head rapidly, side to side. "No, no," he said. "No."

"You're lying, Murray. I can see it in your face. You're trying to feed me a bald-faced lie. Well, it's not going to work. You're terrified of somebody." Tristan got up to pace, but when he put his weight on his right leg, the horrific pain in his calf changed his mind for him. He sat back down as if he'd just thought of more questions.

"You're Catholic, aren't you?" He didn't wait for an answer because he already knew that Murray went faithfully to mass several times a week as well as to Sunday services. "Do you believe in God?"

Murray frowned, but he nodded. "Yes, of course. I'm Catholic most of my life," he said, pulling a rosary out of his pocket and kissing the small crucifix that dangled from the chain. "Of course I believe."

Tristan eyed him. That meant he didn't fear dying. So that wasn't the threat that had him terrified. There was only one other explanation. "Then it's got to be your son."

Murray's eyes went wide as saucers and his sallow complexion turned greenish white. "What? No, no, no, no, no. Where'd you get that? No." But he hurriedly stuck the rosary back in his pocket and wiped his hands on his pants. "No."

"Yes," Tristan said triumphantly. He'd pocketed the rosary because he didn't want to be holding it while he lied. "That's it. They're threatening to harm your son. Where is Patrick now?"

Suddenly, the fisherman was no longer a threat to Tristan or Sandy or Boudreau. He'd turned into a worried father. Tears streamed from his eyes as he shook his head, back and forth. Back and forth. "They have him. I don't know where. They kill him if I don't do what they say. I can't… I can't do it."

Tristan sighed. Kidnappers had Murray's son and were using him to force Murray to spy on Sandy—and for what? He was sure he knew the answer to that question, too.

"Why, Murray? Why did they want you spying on my wife?" he asked, deadly quiet, but when Murray didn't answer right away, Tristan lost the careful control he'd been holding on to with all his strength. He leaped to his feet and slammed his fists down on the table. *"Why?"*

Murray jumped and held up his hands protectively in front of his face. "I don't know," he said. "They just say do it. See where she go, what she do. See who come see." Murray's English was becoming almost impossible to understand. "They say, if I get a chance, go inside and get computers, flash drives, everything I see that's like computers."

Tristan wanted to slap the man and tell him to snap out of it. He needed Murray to calm down. He needed him to think rationally and talk calmly if he was going to find out anything about the people who wanted him dead so badly.

Tristan straightened, took another deep breath and drank a big swallow of the cold water Sandy had finally set in front of him. After the anger that was burning in him had decreased to a flicker, he spoke to Murray again. "What did they tell you about Sandy or me?"

Murray spread his hands. "Nothing. Just say do what they tell me or they kill Patrick."

"Give me your phone."

"No. Can't. Can't. They kill me I don't bring back picture—" Murray suddenly turned frightfully pale. He looked as though he might pass out.

"Picture?" Tristan repeated. "What picture?"

The fisherman's head started shaking back and forth again. He moaned. "Didn't mean to say that," he wailed.

"So sorry, Mr. DuChaud. So sorry. Shame, shame on me." Murray's entire body seemed to deflate. He hung his head and his voice sounded broken. "I tell them about you. No choice. They have my son." He spread his hands, then clasped them in front of his chest.

"Tell me what you told them," Tristan said, working to keep his voice even.

"I say I see you. Say maybe it Tristan DuChaud. Maybe not. But pretty sure. They give camera. Take picture. Get proof. No more spy on Mrs. DuChaud. Watch to get picture, or they kill Patrick. They kill him."

Get proof. So whoever ordered him dead had learned from Cho that he was still alive and they sent him back here to get proof. He'd be happy, more than happy, to oblige. "It's okay, Murray. You did good. I'll be glad to give them what they want."

Boudreau shot him a look. "What you got in that head of yours, boy?"

Tristan ignored him for the moment. He clasped Murray's shoulder and squeezed. "Murray, will you do what I tell you? If you will, I'll do my best to save your son. I can't promise you that I'll be successful, but I can promise that I'll give it my all. My wife is pregnant. I'm going to have a son—" His throat closed up. He swallowed hard. "A son of my own. So I can understand a little of what you're going through."

Murray studied Tristan a long time. Then he straightened. The frightened little man who wouldn't look him in the eye, who'd tried to run, whose perfect English had deteriorated to the point that he was almost not understandable, had transformed again.

This time, the man who straightened was a father,

still scared and worried, but ready to stand up to anyone for his child's sake. "I'll do anything to save my boy."

Tristan stared at him. Nothing Murray had said so far had affected him as much as watching him gather strength and determination in the face of terror over his son's safety. But all the courage the man was able to gather was not enough to erase the desperation in his eyes—the overwhelming fear for his son's life.

And seeing that, Tristan knew exactly how he felt. When he'd first fallen off the oil rig, he'd been convinced he was going to die. He'd thought about Sandy and their baby. In those moments, he'd known he would never see his wife again or ever get a chance to meet his child.

Was that a part of his hell, he'd wondered? The agony of being separated from Sandy and their child? Then he'd thought of the utter emptiness and desolation his life would become if something happened to her, and he had decided yes. That would be the worst hell imaginable.

An understanding took seed and grew inside him. That's how it had been for Sandy, when she'd found out he was dead. A small inkling of why she had been and still was so angry with him—not for staying away, but for not letting her know.

But she wasn't just angry. He remembered the look on her face, in her eyes, when she'd discovered him in the house. She'd been talking to the baby. Even when she recognized him, her hands had wrapped protectively around her tummy. She was keeping her baby safe—even from him.

There had not been one tiny shred of happiness in her eyes. She hadn't been glad to see him.

Had she started to get over him? The thought hit his heart like a physical blow. He felt the anger building again. Anger at himself, yes, but also anger at her. She'd begun to let go. She'd begun to move on. She had begun to make a family out of herself and her unborn child. The pain in his heart nearly doubled him over.

"Tristan?" Boudreau said. "The phone?"

Tristan blinked. Boudreau had called his name more than once. With difficulty, he brought his thoughts back to the problem at hand, finding out who had threatened Murray. He looked at the fisherman then at Boudreau. His Cajun friend held out his hand. He was holding a cell phone.

"What's this?" Tristan asked.

Murray glanced at Boudreau.

Boudreau's brows raised. "Where you been the past few seconds?" he asked.

Tristan sent Boudreau an irritated look, then turned to Murray. "The kidnappers gave this to you?"

He nodded. "To take picture with. They say it better than my phone."

"What can you tell me about them?"

Murray was close to panicking again. "Big men. Maybe American, maybe not. I don't know. I press record button on my phone last time they called."

"You recorded them?" Tristan perked up. A recording. "Good for you." Maybe something on there would reveal who had ordered his death and had masterminded the smuggling operation. "Play it." He held the phone out to Murray.

"Not that phone." Murray pulled a phone from his pocket. "That phone for picture. I recorded them on my phone, the one they call me on."

"Fine. Just play the recording."

"I don't know how. Patrick handles these electronic

devices. All I did, I saw the record button and hit it. I haven't tried to listen." Murray was calming down again and his English was getting better.

Tristan took Murray's phone and looked at it for a moment, pressed a couple of buttons to access internal settings and help, then pressed a few more. He heard Murray's voice, pleading with someone.

"—but the storm was too bad."

"The storm was too bad for you to perform a simple task to save your son's life? I guess that's it, then. Hey, get the kid ready. Say goodbye to your boy, Mr. Cho."

"No, wait!"

Cho's voice coming through the phone's speaker was agonized and broken. Tristan saw a reflection of that pain and fear etched in Murray's face.

"For what, Murray? Till pigs fly? Because it looks like that's how long it's going to take you to finish your task. Well, we don't have that long. Hey, Farrell? Where's the kid? There he is. Settle back and listen, Murray. You're going to get an earful of what happens when you don't do what you're told."

In the background a young male voice cried out in pain once, twice. It was sudden, awful pain, from the sound of his agonized cries.

Murray moaned as his voice on the phone choked out another plea. *"No. Please. Let me talk to him. I swear, I can do it."*

"We don't have time for this, Mr. Cho. If you can do it, why haven't you done it already?"

"Dad! Da-a-ad." The boy went into a coughing fit. *"Come—get me. Please! I'm scared."*

"Patrick!"

Tristan gritted his teeth. The love and fear were so

evident in their voices. He glanced at Sandy, who was looking down and rubbing her hand across the side of her belly. She looked like a Madonna, her goodness shining like a halo. And he knew what he had to do.

He wanted to watch their baby grow up. He wanted to feel that much love for his son, but not through a cloud of fear. He swore to himself that he would not allow Murray's son—or his own—to end up as a casualty of this mess.

"Patrick! Be brave." Through the phone, Murray sucked in a deep breath. *"Don't hurt my boy. I've got something else. Information you will want, but first you have to let Patrick go."*

The man's laughter echoed through the phone line. *"You're ordering us? That is not how it works. You're a little confused. We give the orders. You follow them. Hey, here's a bargain for you. You tell me what you've got, and if it's good enough, maybe we'll let your son live. That's a sale you can't afford to miss."*

Murray put his hand over his mouth and tried to stifle a sob. "I'm sorry," he whispered, looking up at Tristan. "I had to. He's my son."

Through the phone's speaker, Tristan heard Murray take a deep breath. *"It was so dark, except for lightning."* In his fear, Murray's smooth English was breaking down. *"I get close as I could, but when lightning finally light up long time, I see Mrs. DuChaud, and a man."*

"A visitor?" the man said.

"No, no," Murray replied. *"It was dark, but lightning was bright. I think it was Tristan DuChaud."*

"What? Are you serious? Because if you think you can fool us into letting your kid go—"

"No. I see what I see. Maybe it's him. Maybe not. But I know Mr. DuChaud. The man look like him. A lot."

"Could have been a relative. Stop wasting our time."

"A relative? You mean like cousin or brother? No, no. You don't get it. Here's the rest of the story. Mrs. DuChaud and him got very close. Closer than cousin. They were kissing—not like relatives."

"Kissing? I'll be a sonofabitch," the kidnapper said, then muttered under his breath.

Tristan couldn't understand him. He paused and backed up the recording, then played it again.

"—not like relatives."

"I'll be a sonofabitch."

Tristan held his breath, but he still couldn't quite make out the kidnapper's muttered words. "Do you know what he said right there?"

Murray shrugged. "'Got to get proof. Lee will want proof.'"

"Lee? He said Lee?" Excitement coursed through Tristan's blood. Vernon Lee was the owner and CEO of Lee Drilling, the multibillion-dollar corporation that owned a lot of a whole lot of things, including several thousand oil rigs around the world and a large number of land drilling operations. Murray shrugged, and Tristan grabbed his shoulder. "He said *Lee*? Are you sure?"

Murray shrank away from Tristan's hand. "He said it in English. I'm pretty sure."

Lee will want proof. His suspicion had been right all along. He'd known from the start that the man on the satellite phone giving orders to the captain had to be high enough in Lee Drilling, the company that owned the *Pleiades Seagull*, to expect the captain to obey him without argument.

Whether that official was Lee himself, Tristan hadn't known—until now. Now he had some corroboration that who'd ordered Sandy watched and Murray's son kidnapped was the same man who had ordered his death on the *Pleiades Seagull*.

The popular media classified Lee as practically a recluse who fiercely and expensively protected his privacy.

The implications of exposing the multibillionaire were stunning. Even a rumor suggesting that he had masterminded the smuggling of automatic handguns into the United States with the idea of arming criminals and kids with the lethal weapons could destroy him and decimate his multibillion-dollar corporation.

Tristan started the recording back up.

"—want you to do now. You get back over there. Get me proof that the man you saw is Tristan DuChaud. A photo or video. And you'd better not be seen. My boss is smart and thorough and he's got all the money in the world. He'll know a fake within seconds. And trust me, Cho, anything suspicious happens and your kid's dead. Just get me that photo."

"I'll get you the photo. Then what?" Murray's voice was toneless. *"What about my son?"*

"Well, Mr. Cho, you turned out to have something that just might be useful. If you improve how you follow directions and you bring us proof that the man you saw is DuChaud, maybe you can save your son." The man hung up.

Tristan stared at the phone for a moment, reviewing the information he'd just gained. *If* Murray was right and the man had said *Lee*, and if things went perfectly, Tristan just might be able to bring an end to the nightmare of the past two months.

SANDY FELT COMPLETELY at loose ends while Boudreau and Tristan were deciding what to do about Murray, so she decided to cook, if there was enough gas for the portable stove, that was. She checked the can and found that it was over half-full.

She found a couple of cans of chicken stock in the cabinet, along with a small can of cooked chicken. She put the broth and the chicken in a pan. While it was simmering on one burner of the portable stove, she made a roux out of flour and oil on the second burner, then added the South Louisiana holy trinity of cooking— onion, peppers and celery—to it.

Once the vegetables were cooked perfectly, she added them and some sliced andouille sausage from the freezer, a few herbs and some cayenne pepper to the pot. Finally, a can of boiled okra and a can of tomatoes went into the mix.

Tristan came in about the time the pot began simmering. He took a deep breath. "Mmm, gumbo," he said, smiling at her. "When will it be ready?"

Sandy set her mouth and shook her head. "There's not enough for everybody," she said.

"That's okay. Boudreau and Murray have gone to his cabin. I'm headed up there in a few minutes."

"You're going to Boudreau's? Again? Why? He can handle Murray without your help." She sighed. "You are unbelievable."

He frowned. "What? What did I do?"

"What did you do?" She tossed the metal spoon she was holding into the sink, where it clattered against the porcelain. "Are you saying you don't know? You dismissed me with a wave of your hand. You essentially told me to shut up. Then you ignored me. Not to mention you almost killed yourself running after him. Boudreau could have caught him in half the time. And I saw Boudreau's face. He was as worried about you as I was. And you—" She barely stopped for breath.

"I don't know. You're not the same person you were the last time I saw you." She threw down the dishrag she'd tossed over her shoulder while she was cooking. "I'm not sure I know you anymore and I'm not sure I like this new person very much."

Tristan listened to Sandy tick off all the things she was upset about. He'd known she was boiling mad, but he was expecting to be chastised for running, not for failing to take care of himself. Then when he'd smelled the gumbo, he'd had the fleeting fantasy that she wouldn't harangue him at all, that she'd be too worried about him to be angry.

But no such luck. She'd never cut him any slack and she wasn't now. And he knew she was right.

He wasn't the man he had been. He knew that. He had wanted to fully recuperate before he saw her, hoping that she wouldn't notice any difference in him.

But that had been a forlorn hope. She would never have missed the scar on the left side of his head, where the roughneck's bullet had barely missed blowing his brains out, or his deformed right calf, which had only half the muscles it ought to have.

But in his heart, Tristan knew those weren't the things that made him so different.

He'd stared death in the face. He knew what it felt like to be ripped away from everyone and everything he loved. He'd been through the strange and horrible experience of waking up to find himself still alive, in a body that was not the body he remembered, not the body that could do all the things that had been second nature to him.

This body couldn't walk, could barely hold itself upright, it was so weak and clumsy. His whole life, he had defined himself in terms of what he could do. He'd been the best at everything—the best swimmer, the best runner, the best wide receiver. He'd not made the best grades in school, but he'd never had to study to get by.

Then, when his father had been killed on an oil rig and he'd had to give up veterinary school and go to work on the rigs to support his mom and sister and Sandy, his brand-new wife, it had been a huge blow, because it was the first time he'd ever been forced to do something he hadn't wanted to.

From that moment, it had seemed his life had evolved into a dull routine of things he'd never wanted to do.

"Tristan?" Sandy touched his arm.

"What?" he said automatically, then realized he'd been staring into space. He looked at his wife with her T-shirt stretched over her small baby bump and spattered with gumbo and her hair drooping into her eyes.

He'd never seen her when she didn't look adorable and this was no exception. Even spattered with grease and gumbo, with her face bright pink from the heat of the gas stove, she was pretty and cute and glowing. His gaze returned to her tummy. He stepped closer and spread his hand over the rounded shape of their child, growing inside her.

"You're so beautiful," he said.

She lifted her face to his and kissed him. "And you look awful. You need to eat and rest."

"I'll eat later. I have to get to Boudreau's. They're

going to take a photo of me that proves I'm alive. Where's today's newspaper?"

Her face set into the stony expression that told him she disapproved of what he was doing. "Still outside, I'm sure. Tristan, I can take your picture."

He shook his head. "Don't wait on me to eat. It's probably going to take all day to get that picture and get it to the kidnappers. I'll eat some of Boudreau's roast pig."

"Why don't you take the gumbo to Boudreau's, if you don't want—"

"No. Stay inside, Sandy. Just to be safe. I'll be back before dark."

He stalked out and slammed the French doors behind him. He winced at the rattle of glass panes. He hadn't meant to slam the door on her while she was talking, but he couldn't say he was really sorry. He was sick and tired of being sick and tired. He couldn't deal with Sandy right now, because he had no idea how to explain the way he'd been acting toward her.

Besides, if he was going to have a prayer of catching Vernon Lee, and saving Murray's son, he had to get the picture taken and send Murray on his way to turn it over to the kidnappers.

Chapter Nine

"This is a stupid idea," Tristan growled as he shifted his weight off his bad leg while trying to hold the newspaper up so the date was visible. "There's a date and time stamp on the camera. Why isn't that enough?"

"Might be enough, but it ain't dramatic. That man needs to know you know what he's doing, yeah," Boudreau said. "Now stand still." He frowned and squinted at the phone he held in one large hand.

"It's the icon that looks like a camera," Tristan said, unable to keep from chuckling at his friend's efforts to press the minuscule touch screen with his large, bony fingers. He heard the clicking noise that signaled that a photo had been taken.

"Oh, no," he said, the laugh fading. He tossed the newspaper down and reached for the phone. "Give me that. I'm not sending that SOB a photo with me laughing."

But Boudreau held on to it, tapping on the screen. "It's in focus," he said. "Only good one we've gotten, with you fidgeting so much, you."

"It would have been easier if you weren't trying to press the button with those gigantic ham-hands."

Boudreau's face creased into what Tristan knew was

a smile, although someone who didn't know Boudreau might think his expression was murderous.

"Humph," Boudreau huffed, holding up his hands. "These ham-hands saved you in that water. You were caught on a branch so big I almost couldn't break it."

"I was lucky that you were fishing in that inlet that day," Tristan said. He felt a pang in the middle of his chest. Boudreau had been like a father to him all his life, especially after his own dad was gone. And he'd happened to be in just the right place at the right time to save his life. Tristan scowled at the older man.

"What?" Boudreau said grumpily, then turned toward the sink. "I got to make some coffee,"

"Boudreau, what were you doing fishing in that inlet that morning? You don't like it there. You always said it was too close to the rigs. That the discharge from the oil rigs collected there and ruined the fish. You said not even the sharks would eat them."

Boudreau filled the pan with water and put it on the gas stove and lit it. "Probably why you still alive, you."

"You knew, didn't you? Someone told you that night that I'd gone overboard and you figured if the oil from the rigs ended up there, that a dead body might, too."

"That little wife of yours walked up here to tell me. She said I should know. Said I was family." Boudreau's voice faltered at the end.

"So you were looking for me." Now Tristan's voice cracked. It was overwhelming and humbling to think about Sandy and Boudreau, these two people who loved him, who, together, had created the miracle that saved his life.

The gratitude and love that erupted from deep inside him was too much. It filled up his heart and overflowed.

Sandy, in the midst of her grief and pain, had thought about Boudreau. She understood that he needed to know what had happened. He shook his head, trying to stop the stinging behind his eyes. "You went out there to look for me."

Boudreau spent a full minute adjusting the flame under the pan of water, although it appeared to Tristan to be perfect. "I didn't want you getting torn up on the branches and driftwood, or dragged out to sea."

A lump so large he couldn't swallow past it blocked Tristan's throat. He could never repay either his friend or his wife for what they'd done.

He picked the phone up off the table where Boudreau had left it and moved the photo from the phone's memory to the SIM card, then took the card out and placed it in a small manila envelope, which he sealed and set on the table.

"Coffee?" Boudreau asked.

"Only if it can walk over here by itself."

Boudreau chuckled. "It's been boiling awhile. It might do it. Do you want to take some to Murray?"

"Sure." Tristan pushed himself to his feet. His leg was hurting like a sonofabitch after this morning's chase. His body was achy and stiff, as though he hadn't gotten a wink of sleep for days.

"You all right?" Boudreau asked as he handed him two steaming mugs.

Tristan nodded, but he knew he'd groaned when he'd put weight on his leg, and he knew it was going to be painful to walk. "Just a little stove up from this morning."

"Tell Murray he'd better drink up, 'cause as soon as I clean up, we'll be going."

Tristan stopped at the door. "Boudreau…"

"*Mais non.* We have had this talk already, and it's barely past noon. You with that gimpy leg, you'd slow us down. Anyhow, oughtn't you be back home with your wife? What happened to all your worry that she was in danger?"

"Didn't you tell me you thought she was safe?" Tristan muttered.

Boudreau didn't say anything. He just gazed at Tristan.

"Anyhow, Murray said the kidnapper told him to leave her alone. I'm sending Lee proof that I'm alive. He has no reason to go after her now." Boudreau's head bobbed up and down slowly. Was he agreeing or thinking?

Tristan headed outside and found Murray where they'd left him earlier, his hands tied separately and loosely around a tree trunk so he had some range of movement. The fisherman had been working on the knots, but apparently had given up and gone to sleep. He didn't stir until Tristan nudged him with his shoe.

"What? Patrick—" Murray jerked awake. "Oh." He looked around for a few seconds, until he remembered where he was. He lifted his gaze to Tristan's with a carefully blank expression.

"I don't understand why you have to tie me up," he said. "You're going to help me find my son. Why would I run away?"

Tristan shrugged. "You did before. Here's coffee," he said, setting it on the ground between them.

He still didn't trust Murray. For all he knew the fisherman would kick out and try to trip him, and he didn't want to take any risks with his bad leg. "Boudreau says drink up. You two are heading out soon."

Murray reached for the coffee and blew on its surface, then took a cautious sip. "What time is it? Where's my phone? The kidnappers should have called by now."

"Yeah, see," Tristan said, "there's no cell service here. I mean, look around. It's a jungle and a swamp. You'll hear their message when you're on your way to Gulfport."

"They're going to kill Patrick if I'm not there when they get there."

"Don't worry. You'll be back at your trailer in plenty of time. Boudreau will tell you exactly what you're supposed to say and do."

Tristan propped himself against the old rough-hewn bench and drank his hot, strong coffee as he watched Murray until Boudreau came out with a washbasin and tossed the water into the side yard, then set the basin down. He was freshly shaved and he had his shotgun with him.

He did the same trick he had at the house, loosened Murray's bonds with a simple flick of his wrist, leaving the fisherman staring bewilderedly at the ropes he'd tried unsuccessfully to loosen.

"See this gun?" Boudreau asked Murray. "She don't have no compunction about shooting somebody who's not being smart. And she ain't sure how smart you are."

"I'll do just what you say, Mr. Boudreau. I want my boy back. I don't want him hurt. I'm a smart man, Mr. Boudreau. Mr. DuChaud." Murray looked desperate. Given that it had been several days since he'd seen his son, Tristan couldn't blame him.

"Well?" Boudreau said, looking at Tristan, who frowned. "You never did tell me what you're going to do."

"I'd like to go with you."

Boudreau shook his head. "I told you no. You'll slow us down. Go back to your house. Be with your wife."

He gestured to Murray. "Let's go. We got to walk down to the dock and then to the seafood warehouse parking lot to get to Murray's pickup."

Once they were gone, Tristan ducked into Boudreau's cabin and grabbed the automatic handgun that his friend had hidden behind a loose board.

The board covered a hiding place Boudreau had shown Tristan years and years before.

If you ever get in trouble, Boudreau had told him, *behind this board is everything you need.*

And Boudreau had not been exaggerating. Doing a quick inventory, Tristan saw the large magazine for the gun, matches and lighter, a windup flashlight and a battery-operated one, and five hundred dollars in fives and twenties.

Tristan remembered what Boudreau had told him about the stash. *If you're in so much trouble that this ain't enough, then God help you, because I can't.*

"Thanks, Boudreau," Tristan muttered as he pocketed what he needed. The gun for sure, the ammo, the lighter and all the cash. "I'm good for it," he muttered, rising.

He passed the walking stick propped by the door, almost reaching for it but not. He couldn't keep depending on it. Besides, he was probably going to need both hands.

Tristan pocketed everything but the gun. He looked behind the door and found a hunting vest of Boudreau's. With the gun and the large magazine in it, the pockets were a little bulky, but it worked.

He made his way to the dock and across to his garage, where his Jeep was parked. It probably hadn't been driven since he'd gone into the water. Luckily, it started right up.

As he pulled out onto the road, he saw Sandy at the French doors, but he didn't stop. He had to get to Gulfport, where Murray and Boudreau were meeting the kidnappers to hand over the photo.

He and Boudreau had talked about what might happen once the kidnappers got their hands on the card that contained the photo of Tristan holding the newspaper. Both of them were afraid they would kill Murray and his son.

That was why Boudreau was going with Murray and it was part of the reason Tristan was determined to be there, despite Boudreau's objection. Neither Murray nor his son would die if he had anything to do with it.

Tristan caught up to Murray's truck about two miles from the Gulfport commercial pier. He stayed well behind the old vehicle.

Finally, Murray slowed and stopped in front of an RV park across from the pier. Tristan pulled in behind an SUV and watched as Murray got out, unlocked the door of a small recreational vehicle and went inside.

"Go, Boudreau," Tristan said under his breath. "They could be waiting for him inside." But he didn't have to worry. Boudreau waited no more than a few seconds before he got out. He had the shotgun in a seaman's ditty bag.

Tristan slipped out of the Jeep and circled around to the back side of the RV. The small camper was hardly big enough for two people, so he wasn't sure what the kidnappers were going to do.

Truthfully, he didn't know what he was going to do, either, except for one thing. He'd decided a mere picture of him holding a newspaper wasn't good enough to send to the man who'd ordered him killed. He planned to send him a video that proved in no uncertain terms that he was alive.

With Murray's recording of the kidnappers, Tristan

was at least one step closer to finding the man who'd wanted him murdered. If the kidnapper had said *Lee*, then the step was a huge one.

Now he needed to get the flash drive he'd hidden in the nursery, in a shiny blue mobile Sandy had hung over the bed. She'd told him she'd bought blue as good luck, because he'd been sure the baby was a boy.

If the voice on Captain Poirier's satellite phone ordering the commission of traitorous crimes against the United States was proven to be Vernon Lee's, the multibillionaire mogul was about to crash and burn.

He hadn't had a chance to listen to all the conversations he'd captured. With any luck, the captain had called Lee by name at least once.

Tristan wanted to confront Lee in person so he could identify his voice, but if he had to settle for sending the man a video, so be it.

It was around three o'clock and the pier and the RV park were essentially deserted. Murray had told them that most of the slips held fishing boats and fishermen were up and out at sunrise and didn't return until sunset, leaving the dock and the RV park almost empty during midafternoon.

So the kidnappers had chosen the perfect time for their meeting with Murray.

Tristan leaned against the hot metal side of the camper and tried to look casual as he waited to see how the kidnappers were going to contact Murray.

Within moments, he heard a telephone ringing inside, through the obviously thin walls. When Murray answered, Tristan could hear him plainly.

"Hello," Murray said anxiously. "Hello?" After listening for a brief moment, he said, "Wait. Which slip?"

Tristan straightened, hardly daring to breathe so he wouldn't miss a word.

"Forty-two? Did you say forty-two? Oh. Forty-three." Murray paused. "Yes, yes. Of course I have it. I said I would. Is my son there? Hello?"

They'd hung up on Murray, but Tristan had the slip number. He only hoped it was Slip 43 at *this* pier.

He took off at a gimpy run, needing to make it as far away as he could from Murray's RV before he and Boudreau came out.

Boudreau could possibly be angry enough at him to fill his butt full of bird shot if he saw him. By the time he reached the Jeep and dared to take a look back at Murray's camper, Boudreau and Murray were hurrying toward the pickup. Boudreau said something to Murray on the way and Murray responded by pointing east across the rows and rows of slips that made up the docks of the commercial pier.

Tristan climbed into the Jeep and pulled out into traffic. He drove well past the general area that Murray had pointed out and parked in a loading zone. If his Jeep got towed, he'd deal with it after he'd dealt with the kidnappers.

When he got out of the Jeep, his leg nearly gave way. It was throbbing with pain and the little muscle he had left quivered with fatigue and weakness. He probably had only a few seconds' lead on Murray and Boudreau, so he quickly scanned the docks until he saw the row of slips that included number 43. Reaching into the rear seat of the Jeep, he pulled out an old baseball cap and a rag he kept in the backseat to wipe his windshield.

As he walked carefully down the dock toward Slip 43, which held a relatively small fishing boat, he put the cap on, pulling it down to shadow his face, then he shook out the rag and mopped the back and front of his neck and then his face, just about the time he passed the slip. If the kidnappers were waiting for him somewhere nearby, he didn't see them, but then he'd limited his vision greatly by holding the rag over his face as he passed.

Slips 44 and 45 were empty, so Tristan stopped at Slip 46, which held a houseboat. After taking off the bulky hunting vest and hiding it behind a coil of rope, he stepped onto the deck of the houseboat and hid, waiting to see who showed up at Slip 43. He thought Murray and Boudreau would be walking down the pier by now, but maybe Boudreau was checking out the area, too, before he let Murray expose himself.

The houseboat rocked a little and Tristan had to steady himself when his leg protested. Then, at the same instant he realized there was someone behind him, he felt a gun barrel in the middle of his back.

"What the hell are you doing on this boat?" a gruff voice said.

"What?" Tristan said, his voice high-pitched as if he were terrified. "What are you doing? What's that?" He tried to turn around, but the pressure in the middle of his back increased.

"Don't move, bud, if you know what's good for you," the gruff voice said.

"I—I'm not. I mean I won't. I mean—"

"Shut up," the man snapped. "Now, what's going on here? Who sent you?"

"No-nobody sent me," Tristan stammered, trying to sound genuinely afraid. He was, a little. After all, the man had a gun stuck in his back and his weapon was on the other side of the dock. The only thing that would make the situation worse at this moment would be if Murray and Boudreau showed up.

He glanced down the pier, but didn't see anybody— yet.

"I swear. I was just hiding here, waiting for…" He stopped, his mind suddenly blank. What could he say? What would sound reasonable enough and at the same time slightly ridiculous?

He'd like to make the man think he was harmless if he could. Then he had it. Or at least the beginning of it. A story that just might work.

"See," he said breathlessly, "my wife's screwing the guy that owns that boat down there." He pointed vaguely in the direction of Slip 43, then tried to turn around to face the man, as probably anyone would do if they hadn't quite figured out that what was sticking into their back was a gun barrel.

"Don't! Move!" the man said, sounding as though he were gritting his teeth.

"O-okay. Sorry. Anyway, she told me she was going shopping, but I think she's coming over here with who-ever owns that boat. I found a note in her purse that said Slip 43, Gulfport pier. I'm sure this is it."

The man cursed, long and colorfully. "Get the hell off this boat," he ordered Tristan, "and keep going until you're off the pier."

"But they're probably on their way. They might see me. I don't want her to see me. And I sure don't want him to. Not till I'm ready."

Tristan felt the pressure of the gun barrel ease. Had he done it? Had he convinced the man that he was harmless?

"Get off the boat, now!"

"But I need to—" Tristan didn't have to come up with

what he needed to do because the man grabbed his arm and turned him around, right into a big right fist.

Tristan went down like a rock. He was barely conscious and he tasted blood, but the man wasn't done with him. He picked him up bodily by the neck of his shirt and the back belt loop of his jeans and tossed him off the boat. Tristan's shoulder hit the deck hard. He rolled a couple of times, coming to an abrupt stop against the coil of rope where he'd hidden his weapon. His cheek scraped against the rough wood of the deck.

While he lay there, trying to gather enough sense back into his head to figure out which way was up, he heard Murray, about forty feet away, probably at Slip 43, saying he had a SIM card with a photo of Tristan DuChaud on it.

Tristan tried to clear his vision. He blinked and rubbed his eyes, but it didn't help. Meanwhile his tongue was exploring the bloody cut on his lip. He blinked again and this time, he saw something.

He was lying on the pier directly across from the houseboat, and although he was inclined to doubt what he saw, he decided to believe it, because if what he saw was real, then he and Boudreau and Murray might make it away from here alive.

As he watched, Boudreau silently paddled a dinghy up beside the houseboat and reached up to catch one of the tie lines and haul himself up onto the deck, his shotgun slung over his shoulder.

When he saw Tristan he made a face and shook his head. Then he held up the shotgun and pointed to Tristan, looking a question.

Tristan nodded and pulled the vest from behind the rope. Boudreau nodded, then gestured toward Murray. Tristan lifted his head enough to take a look at the odds.

Murray was, at best, half the size of the two men who were towering over him. One of them had to be the man who had coldcocked Tristan.

He looked back at Boudreau and read the Cajun's gestures as clearly as if he were talking. *I'll go first and get the drop on them. You follow. Tell Murray to run, and you and me can tune those two giants up a bit.*

Tristan frowned, pointed in the direction of his leg and shrugged, hoping Boudreau could read his answer in impromptu hand signals. *Maybe you. Probably not me.*

Boudreau stepped onto the pier and cocked his double-barreled shotgun. The two big, strapping blond men froze, then slowly turned and eyed the weapon. One of them held a pistol in his hand.

"Drop it or I'll make a sieve outta you," Boudreau said.

The man looked at the shotgun, then at his handgun.

"Throw the guns in the water," Boudreau added, lifting his weapon.

"What?"

"I don't like killing," Boudreau said. "But when I got to, I make a good job of it. I'll start with your legs, yeah." He pointed the gun at the man's legs and slid his finger across both triggers.

"Okay," the man said quickly. "We don't want no trouble. We got business with Mr. Cho."

Tristan pushed himself to his feet with all the strength he could muster. Just as he pulled the handgun from the vest, he heard something from inside the houseboat. It sounded like a muffled voice crying out. But he didn't have time to check it out because Boudreau needed him.

"Business about a photo?" Tristan said, finding it a little hard to speak around his swelling lip.

The man looked at him. "I knew you weren't quite as dumb as you sounded."

"And I knew you were," Tristan responded. "Murray, take your phone out and hit the video record button. And don't screw up."

Murray frowned, but he did as he was told. He held up the phone and started recording.

But Tristan wasn't nearly as interested in showing off for Lee as he had been. He'd taken an awful chance, following Boudreau and Murray out here, and he knew he'd hear about it from Boudreau later. So he just walked around until he could put his face in the middle of the phone's screen with the two kidnappers in the frame behind him.

"Hello, Mr. Lee. I'm Tristan DuChaud. I'm giving you plenty of footage here, so you have time to get a match for my face. Sorry about the cut on my lip. That shouldn't hinder the face-matching software much. I want you to know that I'm alive and mostly well, and that I'm looking forward to meeting you. I'd like to have the opportunity to shake the hand of the man who tried to kill me."

He smiled. "I won't do it. I wouldn't touch you with a ten- or even a hundred-foot pole. But I do want to stand in the same room with you and choose not to shake your hand. You are the lowest piece of scum on the planet, and another thing I'd love to do is shoot you in cold blood, but I won't do that, either. I'm going to let the international court deal with you, you traitor, you subhuman, you piece of slime under my boot."

He wiped a drop of blood that he could feel trickling down his chin. Then he smiled again. "By the way, if you even think about sending anyone near my wife again, I might just have to change my mind about touching you.

I won't be shaking your hand, though. Have a nice day, Mr. Lee." He made a throat-slicing motion at Murray, who looked down to find the stop-recording key.

"Give it to me," Tristan said, and Murray complied again. Tristan held up the phone. "Here you go, boys. Take that to your boss and tell him Tristan DuChaud says he hopes he enjoys the show." He looked behind them at Boudreau. "You going to shoot them?"

"No!" Murray cried. "They know where my son is. Please!"

Boudreau shook his head. "Shells are pretty expensive these days. Reckon I might opt for a cheaper alternative. Say—" Instead of finishing his sentence, Boudreau took one step forward and shoved one of the men hard into the other one.

Both of them teetered for a second, then tumbled from the pier into the water.

Tristan grinned at him, then looked down to where the two men were splashing about. "Hey, boys, I'm going to put the phone right here. Mr. Lee will be looking for this. You'd better get dried off and get it to him. Once he sees that I'm alive and well, tell him to come and see me. My wife and I are getting reacquainted, so please call first." Tristan made a show of getting ready to walk away, then he remembered the noise he'd heard in the houseboat. He stopped and looked at Murray.

"Murray, I think your son's in the houseboat. Boudreau, you want to keep an eye on these guys while Murray and I check it out?

"Sure," Boudreau said.

"Come on, Murray," Tristan said. "Let's go make sure there are no more muscle heads around and get Patrick out of there."

They made short work of searching the houseboat for another thug. Inside, they found Patrick tied up and strapped to a chair. His face was bruised, but he looked healthy otherwise and he started crying when he saw his dad.

Murray untied his son and got him to his feet, then pulled him close for a long hug. Patrick hugged his father back.

"Patrick, my boy. Are you all right?"

Patrick nodded. "They hit me and kept me tied up," he said brokenly, still crying. "But I'm okay. Oh, Dad, I'm sorry. I forgot to lock the door. I'm sorry."

"Shh," Murray said. "None of this is your fault, son. They'd have broken the door in. I'm just glad they didn't hurt you any…any more than they did." He hugged his son close again.

"Think you can walk?" Tristan asked.

Patrick nodded.

"Let's go. It'll be dark before long and I'd like to get out of here before those guys manage to pull their thousand-dollar suits out of the water."

Tristan led the way back down the dock. The two thugs were wading toward shore, glancing back at Boudreau with every step.

"By the way, guys," Tristan called to them, "tell your boss my number's in the book. Have a nice day." He tipped an imaginary hat.

"Don't get too cocky, son," Boudreau muttered, looking around. "They could have friends."

Tristan smiled at Boudreau. "Not as good a friend as I have."

Chapter Ten

Vernon Lee watched the recording his computer expert had just received and uploaded to the plasma screen. He didn't take his eyes off the screen for the entire one and a half minutes. When it ended with Tristan DuChaud saying, *Have a nice day, Mr. Lee*, Lee growled, "Play it again!"

On the screen, his voice amplified by the state-of-the-art speakers in Lee's media room, Tristan DuChaud said, *Have a nice day, Mr. Lee.*

A shiver of disgust slid through Lee. He didn't like smart-asses, and based on what he'd just seen, DuChaud was definitely a smart-ass. Lee watched the recording a third time.

So this was the man who had overheard him talking to that moron Poirier. The man who, in all likelihood, had copies of those conversations somewhere.

"Back it up to where he says have a nice day," Lee ordered his computer expert. "And freeze it there."

He studied DuChaud. Yep. A smart-ass. "You probably hid it in your house, didn't you?" Lee muttered. "You look like the type to hide it in plain sight." Without taking his eyes off the frozen picture of the man who could bring him crashing down, Lee picked up his phone and dialed a number.

"I'll get rid of that recording and you, smart-ass, with a perfect match." Lee chuckled. "A match. That's a good one."

After giving orders to his employee on the other end of the phone, Lee hung up and watched faces flash by on the screen, too fast to recognize what they were, much less who.

Bored, he stood. "Gartner," he said to his computer expert, "I'll be back in an hour. I'm having dinner with my daughter. Print out the facial matches and have them ready for me to look at."

Charles Gartner turned in his chair.

"Mr. Lee, it will probably take all night for the computer to find every facial match. Your database now contains more than a billion people."

"Did I ask you how long it would take?"

The American blinked, but his gaze didn't waver. "No, sir," he said, his face completely blank of expression.

Lee lifted his chin slightly. "What did I ask you to do?"

"To print out the facial matches for you."

"Do you know why I want that, even though DuChaud told me who he is?"

Gartner swallowed. "Yes, sir. You don't like mistakes or loose ends."

"That's very good, Mr. Gartner. What else don't I like?"

"Smart-asses, sir."

Lee thought he saw, just for an instant, a look of annoyance, maybe even anger, on Gartner's face, but it was gone before he could react to it. "Very good, Mr.

Gartner. Very good. Print them in color, if that's not too much trouble."

"No trouble at all, sir." Gartner turned back to the monitor. He picked up a pen and jotted a note onto his desk calendar.

Lee pushed the door to the penthouse open and went inside, looking forward to having dinner with his daughter.

SANDY WAS TIRED of reading, tired of napping, even tired of eating. She'd heated soup and made herself a grilled cheese sandwich earlier. She glanced at the portable stove and thought about firing it up again and making a cup of tea, but she didn't really want tea that badly.

Pouring a glass of water, she walked over to the French doors, thinking about where Tristan had been going in such a hurry earlier.

She'd heard the Jeep's motor, but by the time she'd gotten to the doors and opened them, he was taking off up the road. It occurred to her that in the past, she'd almost always known exactly where he was and what he was doing. He'd seldom stayed out late with buddies or stopped at the local watering hole for a drink or six.

But today, it had been hours since he'd taken off in the Jeep. He'd promised her he'd be home before dark. Apparently his word wasn't worth squat these days.

The sun was sinking low and the sky was turning pink. It looked as though it was going to be a clear night.

Her restlessness returned. She knew what she wanted to do. She wanted to go for a walk, maybe down to the dock, where she and Tristan had sat on so many evenings like this and watched the sun's reflection in the water until they could no longer see it. But it wasn't the same without him. Nothing was.

Besides, he'd told her to stay inside. Dejected and feeling a little sorry for herself, she watched the sky turn from pink to magenta, then to purple.

It was gloaming, that few minutes right before dark that she disliked so much.

Then, out of the dull palette of dark hues, a bright set of headlights caught her attention. Her stomach flipped, but immediately she recognized the Jeep's headlights and her heart soared like a teenager in the throes of her first crush. She reached for the doorknob to throw the door open and run to him, but as the door swung open, she stopped herself. She actually felt timid about going to him.

Because if he didn't gather her up in his arms, she wasn't sure if she could bear it.

So she waited, her pulse pounding in her ears. She tried to calm her breathing and her heartbeat, but it was no use. She knew she was on the verge of hyperventilating, but she couldn't help it. As he stepped onto the patio the light from the kitchen played on his face and emphasized the deep lines around his mouth and between his brows as he stepped inside.

He looked exhausted and in pain. His face was drawn and pale and his clothes looked two sizes too big. But he was here.

"Tristan," she said softly, the longing inside her reflected in her voice. Then she saw his swollen lip. "What happened?"

His nostrils flared as if he were taking in a deep breath. "Nothing," he muttered, looking down at the floor.

Suddenly, she wanted him so badly her entire body quivered. A desire so deep, so primal that it nearly doubled her over spread through her, and she wanted to grab him and kiss him and mold her body to his and damn the consequences.

But just as she began to lift her arms, his steady, solemn gaze filled with fire and he pulled her to him, so quickly that she lost her footing.

He caught her, wrapping his lean, muscled arms around her and burying his nose in her hair. She could hear and feel his unsteady breaths. He said nothing, just held her, squeezing a little too tightly, which was the perfect amount. She slid her arms around him and hugged him back.

After a long, long time, he lifted his head and kissed her. It was barely a kiss, just a brushing of lips against lips, but it ignited a sweet flame so deep and strong that it disturbed the little bean.

"Oh," she said.

"What?" Tristan whispered hoarsely, his lips still against hers.

"He kicked me. He's getting really good at that."

"Yeah?" His mouth flattened and he glanced down between them.

She took his hand. "Come with me," she said.

"San, I'm tired. This has been a long, long day. I just need to go to bed."

"Lucky for you," she said, "that's where we're going." She tugged on his hand until, with a sigh, he followed her.

In the bedroom, she turned back the covers. "Take off your shirt and sit down. I'll untie your shoes." She crouched down, settling her baby bump onto her lap, untied his sneakers and slid them off, then slid off his socks.

"I ought to take a shower," he said, his voice muffled as he pulled off his shirt.

She looked up at him. "You look clean."

"I bathed at Boudreau's, but still…"

She started to rise and Tristan stood and caught her arms, helping her up.

"I'm not that bad off yet," she said. "I can get up by myself."

He didn't comment as he unbuckled his belt and let his pants drop to the floor.

Sandy went to the other side of the bed and quickly shed her clothes.

"I've got something to show you," she said, climbing under the covers beside him. She lay back against the pillows. "Look." She pushed the covers down to expose her breasts and belly.

Tristan took a swift breath. "Wow," he said.

"I know. I'm huge. The little bean's kicking around in there and making things pretty uncomfortable for me."

Tristan put his hand out, then drew it back.

"It's okay." She caught his hand and placed it, palm down, on her tummy. "Rub right here." She moved his hand to the right side. "The bean likes that."

Tristan's fingers tentatively spread over her skin and she closed her eyes.

The desire was still there, throbbing within her, but her heart was filled with something more now. This was all she'd ever wanted. She and Tristan, together, with their baby. A family, bonded together with such strength of love that nothing could ever tear them apart.

She pressed Tristan's hand against her skin, guiding it back and forth, back and forth, in the spot where the little bean's feet usually were. After a few seconds, she felt a tiny kick from the inside.

"Did you feel that?" she asked.

Tristan turned onto his side. He looked up at her. "That was a kick?"

"Hey, he's not very big yet," she said indignantly.

"How big?"

She held her hands up, about ten inches apart. "And he probably weighs around twelve ounces or so."

"Our little bean," Tristan whispered. "Have you named him already?" He looked up at her.

She shook her head. "I'd wanted us to do that together, and then you— Then I kind of figured that I'd probably name him after you."

Tristan stared at her for a long time, then he pushed up on his elbow and leaned over and kissed her belly. "Hi, little bean," he said softly.

Sandy's breath caught as she watched her husband greeting his child. "You know, the doctor told me he can hear now. He said we should talk to him."

"You've been doing that all along, haven't you?"

Sandy laughed. "Yes."

"Because you talk to everything. The plants, the food, me—even when I'm asleep."

"I cannot deny that I do," she said.

Tristan straightened, still looking at her. "San, I don't know what will happen if I try to make love with you, but I'd like to try."

She touched his face. "I'll do anything you need me to do."

"You may need to be on top. My damn leg won't hold me up very well."

"That won't be a problem," she said.

Tristan pushed himself up until he could reach her mouth and kissed her with all the abandoned ardor of a man who hadn't made love with his wife in more than four months.

She felt him harden against her thigh and thought, as she had the last time they'd almost made love, that if he had trouble it would not be with his virility. Her desire swelled inside her until she ached and pulsed with need. With a moan, she slid down into the bed on her side, facing him.

She leaned over to kiss him and he grimaced. "Oh, you're on your right side," she said. "That's your bad side. Here." She sat up and moved over. "Lie on your back and I'll do the work."

His face turned red. "I don't want it to be like this, San."

"Like what? You're injured so I will take over temporarily, because I do love it when you're above me, my man."

Tristan opened his mouth to protest again, but Sandy bent down and kissed him. She kept on kissing him as she straddled him, feeling his arousal grow harder. She lifted herself onto her knees and let him be the guide as she slowly and carefully lowered herself onto him.

Being filled by her husband was an exquisite pleasure and a pulse-pounding need. Her muscles contracted around him and he groaned and thrust upward, grasping her around the waist and lifting her, his lean, muscled arms straining to hold her suspended while he searched her face for any trace of pain or discomfort.

"I'm wonderful," she said, her voice low and sultry. "Let go. I want to feel you. One hundred percent of you." He did as she asked and she sank down onto him, then began to move.

Tristan made a noise deep in his throat as he took her

by the waist again. She moaned in protest, but it was immediately obvious that he wasn't planning to stop her or slow her down this time.

No, he was controlling the pace, easing them into a deliberately steady rhythm that was not enough for her. She kept trying to rush each thrust, but Tristan held on to her and kept the rhythm steady.

"Tris, let me move," she murmured.

"Don't rush it, San. Keep it slow and steady. In and out. In and out. Feel the sensations. You know how we like it best."

"But it's been so long. I need—"

Tristan leaned up and pulled Sandy to him, until he could reach her breasts with his mouth.

She touched his cheek. "Tris, don't forget about the milk," she said softly.

He took a shaky breath. "I haven't." He closed his mouth over her right breast and ran his tongue across her distended nipple.

"Oh!" she cried, trying to breathe normally, trying to keep it steady and failing. Her back arched to push her breast into his mouth. Then she felt him sucking lightly on the tender tip. She gasped and at the same time, his insistent rhythm sped up, until they were moving together, faster and faster.

His thrusts sent her higher and higher until she was sure she was about to explode into a thousand pieces.

Her jagged flashes of pleasure synced with his thrusts. They breathed in tandem and moved in perfect accord.

Then Tristan thrust harder than he had so far, and he touched something so deep within her that she did explode. Thousands of bright stars burst in front of her vision and thousands more popped and sizzled inside her.

And everywhere they touched, they singed her with another level of pleasure. She had no concept of anything
except the two of them and the culmination of joy they
were sharing.

Much later, Tristan's shoulder moved restlessly under
Sandy's head and she murmured in protest. He turned his
head and pressed a kiss into her hair. "My arm's going
to sleep. Sorry I'm such a wimp."

"You are not," Sandy said, lifting her head enough that
he could slide his arm out. She laid her head back down
on the pillow. "You're injured. You've hardly had time
to recover. That's not a wimp. That's a very brave man."
She stretched and yawned, feeling tiny aftershocks of her
climaxes. She moaned in languid pleasure.

Tristan stretched, too. Sandy watched him, admiring
his lean torso and smooth golden skin. She reached out
to touch his chest, but he suddenly froze for an instant,
then jackknifed, uttering a cry of pain as he reached for
his right leg.

"Tris? What's wrong?" she asked, sitting up to see
what he was doing.

His fingers were gingerly massaging the muscle
that was left on the inside of his calf. His face was distorted into a mask of pain. Sandy reached for him, but he
shrugged away. He was breathing between clenched teeth
and every so often another groan would escape his lips.

She saw the knotted muscles on the inside of his calf.
They were bulging and twisted. This was the first time
she'd seen the damage the sharks had done. The outside
of his calf was horribly disfigured. There was nothing
on there but skin pulled over bone and the scars of ugly,
uneven stitches.

She pressed her lips together to hold back a moan at

what she saw. The muscle that ran along the outside of his right calf had been ripped away by a shark's sharp teeth. There was no imagining the kind of pain he'd endured, and the physical agony had only been part of his suffering. He'd been plunged into dark, murky water filled with sharks. He'd been lucky not to have been sliced in two by the fish's sharp teeth.

"Oh, Tris, how did you stand it?"

He didn't answer her. But she felt a lessening of the tension in his body. The cramps were easing. His fingers relaxed and he leaned back against the pillows. When she dared to peer at his face, it appeared almost relaxed, as well.

"It's stopped hurting?"

He blew out a breath. "It stopped cramping. That's a big deal." He let his head fall back against the pillow. His face was pale, but it was no longer a mask of pain. Within seconds, he was breathing softly and evenly. He was asleep.

Sandy smiled and touched the tip of her finger to the lines in the middle of his forehead. She smoothed them out as lightly and carefully as she could, then she leaned over and kissed him just at the corner of his mouth. He didn't seem to wake up.

She sank down into the bed and settled her head on the pillow. Now that he was no longer in pain, she felt comfortable going to sleep herself.

Tristan was here. She was safe.

Until all hell broke loose.

Chapter Eleven

"What the hell?" Tristan cried, his head filled with what sounded like the howling of the hounds of hell.

"Smoke alarm," she muttered, groaning as she pushed the covers away. "I'll reset it."

"No!" he yelled as he vaulted out of the bed, straightening his right leg carefully. He couldn't have it cramping again. Not now.

"Sandy!" he shouted to be heard over the siren. "Sandy! Get dressed. The house is on fire!"

"What?" She sat up and squinted.

"There." He pointed toward the open door to the hall. Eerie orange and yellow reflections danced on the walls.

She got up and grabbed her jeans. "Oh, my God. I didn't leave the portable stove on, did I?"

"Hurry!" He had his jeans and tennis shoes on. He grabbed his shirt. "Lee did this."

"Lee?" Sandy repeated as she pulled on her jeans and stepped into her Skechers flats.

"The man who tried to have me killed. Stay here. I'm going to see how bad the fire is. And stay away from the windows."

"They're still out there?"

Just as she spoke, a very loud crack split the air, easy to hear above the blaring siren. She screamed.

"Get down!" Tristan yelled.

Sandy immediately dropped to the floor. "Was that a gunshot?" she asked incredulously. "They set fire to the house and now they're *shooting* at us?"

Tristan looked up. The bullet had come in high. It hit just under the crown molding. "Maybe not. That came in really high. Lee may have told them not to kill us."

"Thoughtful of him," Sandy said archly.

Tristan smiled. "I think we'll be okay. The alarm is hooked up to the fire department now, right?"

"No," she said.

"Damn it, I told you to call them and—"

"I did. They couldn't get it to work this far out."

Tristan cursed. "Okay. No problem. *Those guys* don't know it's not hooked up. They're not going to stay around long with the siren blaring like that, *and* I'll bet you Boudreau will open fire any second now."

He heard something, a lower-pitched blast, still loud enough to overcome the siren. "There he is." He walked over to the window.

"Tris? What are you doing? Get away from there."

He didn't answer. He crouched down in front of the window and pulled the automatic pistol out of his jeans. He'd taken off the specially made magazine, so he couldn't use it on automatic, but he could let them know he was armed and dangerous.

He opened fire before he could identify anything to aim at. He aimed low, hoping not to kill anyone. The only person he'd ever killed was the unfortunate roughneck he'd dragged with him into the water on the oil rig. And that had been mostly accidental.

A bullet shattered the upper part of the window and slammed into the wall behind him about a foot above their heads. Maybe they weren't trying to miss them.

"Sandy, lie down on the floor. All the way down." He didn't hear her if she answered him because at that instant a reverberating boom split the air.

It was Boudreau's shotgun. The Cajun had let loose with both barrels. The 12 gauge was an impressive weapon. It's only disadvantages were its weight and how few rounds it held.

Behind him, he heard Sandy say something, but she wasn't talking loud enough.

"What?" he shouted as another slug hit the wall barely a foot above his head. He fired back, still unable to see anything except the darkness and an ever-growing cloud of smoke from the fire. He could smell it now.

"Sandy?" he yelled. "Stay put. Boudreau's out there. This will be over in no time."

She didn't answer.

"San?" he called, just as a slug whistled close to his ear. "Damn it! They are shooting to kill. San? Where are you?"

"I'm right here," she said.

He glanced around and saw her crawling toward the closet.

"Get back behind the bed," he yelled. "What the hell are you doing?"

"I need to get the box with all our photos," she rasped, then coughed. "And all our papers."

"No! You're going to get shot."

"But all our papers will burn up. Our marriage license."

Another slug whizzed past his ear, too close for comfort. "Damn it, Sandy. Get. Down!"

Boudreau's shotgun roared again, its low-pitched boom echoing through the air underneath the squeal of the siren.

Tristan ducked below the edge of the window and looked toward Sandy. She was on the floor, crawling back toward the far side of the bed.

At that instant a barrage of gunfire hit the window, sending shattered glass everywhere.

"Cover your head!" he yelled as he closed his eyes and did the same. Once the gunfire ceased, he eased his head up so he could see out. He saw something fiery red, lighting an arc in the darkness. A flare gun. *God bless Boudreau.*

Tristan heard more gunfire, but it wasn't aimed toward the house this time. They were shooting at Boudreau. Another flare erupted and lit up in the dark.

In the red light, Tristan saw two moving shadows. He opened fire, forgetting his plan to try to avoid killing anyone. These people were shooting at them. They deserved what they got.

He saw the flare stop suddenly and heard a man scream. The flare had hit him square in the torso.

He fired again. "Shoot another one, Boudreau," he muttered. "I need to see." As if he'd heard him, Boudreau fired another flare that lit up the area with eerie red light. Tristan saw a moving shadow bending over, probably checking on his buddy. He aimed and fired and the shadow went down.

Tristan realized he was holding his breath. He blew it out and took a deep breath to replace it. But instead of clean, refreshing air, harsh smoke filled his lungs, throwing him into a painful coughing fit.

By the time he caught his breath, he heard the crunch of footsteps outside the window. He stiffened and aimed his weapon, wondering why he could suddenly hear. Then he realized the siren had stopped. The battery must have run down.

"Tristan!"

It was Boudreau, standing at the window. "Boudreau!" he yelled, triggering another coughing fit. He heard Sandy coughing behind him, too. "Are they down?"

Boudreau nodded. "One dead. One wounded. One running for the truck they came in. Let's go. The house is going up."

"What?"

"You got to get out of there. You're inhaling smoke. Where's your wife?"

"Behind the bed. Sandy?" he called.

"Get her. That fire's out of control."

Tristan turned away from the window. "Sandy, let's go. We've got to climb out the window. Boudreau will help you." He backed toward the door to the hall.

"Where are you going?" Sandy asked.

"Go to the window, San. I'll be right behind you."

He ran out of the bedroom and saw exactly what Boudreau was talking about. The whole front of the house was painted with an odd red-yellow color, swirled about with black. *Fire and smoke.*

He'd been absolutely right when he'd told Sandy there was no time to save belongings. But he had to grab one thing. The flash drive that held the incriminating satellite phone conversations. That was why Lee had resorted to fire. He was determined to destroy any evidence of his involvement.

Shoving the nursery door open, he jerked the blue mobile down from over the bed. As he hurried back to the master bedroom, he felt around on the plastic decoration until he found what he was looking for. A blue rhinestone-studded flash drive in the shape of a baseball glove. He tossed the plastic mobile onto the floor and put the flash drive in his pocket.

Back in the bedroom, Sandy had barely moved. She was trying to get her feet under her, hanging on to a bedpost for balance.

He held out his hand. "Come on. We've got to get out of here. Boudreau's taken care of the bad guys."

She didn't answer. She was almost passed out from the smoke. He pulled her to her feet. "Okay," she wheezed. "I'm fine now." But she was panting for air.

He held out his hand and Sandy took it, squeezing tightly. "Don't be afraid," he said. "I'm right here."

The shallow breaths became coughs. Once she started coughing she couldn't stop, not even long enough to catch her breath.

"Tristan, let's go." Boudreau's head was turned, checking out the area around them. "You got to get her out of there. She's got too much smoke in her lungs."

Tristan took a breath to answer, but all he breathed in was smoke. He started coughing, too.

"*Maintenant.* You both got to be breathing clean air—now!"

Sandy had quit trying. Her limbs were limp. She was exhausted from coughing and from lack of oxygen. He wrapped his arm around her waist to guide her.

"Try to climb up on the windowsill, San. Boudreau, help me. My leg's about to give out on me."

"Sit her up on the sill," Boudreau said.

Tristan managed to lift her by balancing most of his weight on his left leg.

"Do it…myself," she muttered between coughs.

"Okay, Boudreau. Pull her out. She's exhausted."

Boudreau's large hands caught her by the waist and lifted her out through the window.

"Got her!" he called.

Tristan managed to climb through the window, but when he let go and landed on the ground his leg gave way and he fell. His calf muscle cramped and he could do nothing but roll on the grass and massage the knots until the pain eased up.

"Get up, you," Boudreau whispered. "The guy who ran for the truck's coming back. And there's a second man coming behind him."

"Take Sandy and run to my Jeep," Tristan said, massaging the muscle.

"*Non! C'est impossible.* They shot out your tires first thing.

"Sandy's car, then." Tristan pushed himself to his feet.

"They're between us and her car. We'd have a shoot-out in the open and she's in no shape to run." Boudreau kept an eye out for anyone approaching as he talked. "Now get up!" he snapped.

"And do what?" Tristan shot back. "Sounds to me like we're trapped here."

"We've got to find cover. Somebody's gonna notice the smoke and the fire department will come. Meanwhile, we got to hide. Head for the cabin."

Tristan helped Sandy to her feet and held on to her as she had another coughing fit.

"That's a surefire trap. They'll follow us and block the path."

"*Oui*, but, *cher*, we know the swamp. They don't."

A spate of gunfire sounded. Boudreau looked at Tristan and nodded toward the path to the dock, then he headed for the corner of the building. He planned to draw the pursuers' fire while Tristan and Sandy made it into the vines and branches that would hide them from view.

Tristan felt like a coward and a failure, leaving Boudreau to fight alone. But at the same time, his primary goal was to keep Sandy and the baby safe. So he guided her toward the path as quickly as he could, cringing every time he heard a gunshot.

Sandy had finally quit coughing, but fighting the smoke in her lungs had exhausted her. She had more trouble navigating the path than he did. He tried letting go of her, but they were more stable together than apart.

Before they'd been on the path one minute, he heard rifle fire, followed by two shotgun blasts. He stopped, so suddenly that Sandy stumbled. He couldn't bear the thought that he'd left Boudreau back there by himself, fighting men who were probably trained soldiers and who likely had some of the best weaponry available.

But getting Sandy to safety was the most important thing. Wincing at the gunfire, Tristan pulled Sandy close again and headed up the path to Boudreau's house.

"Just a little farther, San."

She nodded doggedly, obviously concentrating on putting one foot in front of the other for long enough to get to the cabin.

He turned her face to his and studied it. Were her lips

turning blue, or was he seeing the combination of soot and the dancing reflections of the fire and smoke? He ran his thumb across her lips, then looked at it. Sure enough, his thumb came away stained with soot.

But the blue tint was still there. Was she that oxygen-deprived? There was no doubt that she was struggling to breathe. If he didn't get some clean air into her lungs and some fresh water for her to drink to wash out the toxins, her lack of oxygen could not only hurt her, it could harm the baby.

He cursed his leg. They should have gotten to the cabin by now. He set his jaw against the pain and tried to increase his speed, hoping Sandy could keep up.

He heard a rustling of the vines and leaves lining the path behind them. He immediately dropped to the ground behind a tree and pulled Sandy down beside him. Retrieving his gun, he waited.

Beside him, Sandy made a small, distressed sound. "Tris, I'm tired—" A strangled cough erupted from her throat. She covered her mouth with both hands, but it didn't help. The coughs kept coming.

"Hang in there, hon," Tristan muttered, wincing at the noise she was making and wondering who—or what—he'd heard moving through the underbrush. "We'll be at Boudreau's in no time. Can you try not to cough?"

She made a guttural sound, a laugh or a groan.

At that instant, the leaves and vines started shaking and someone stepped into the path. Tristan stiffened and tightened his hand on the gun's trigger, but it was Boudreau.

He breathed a sigh of relief and stood. Boudreau looked startled to see them.

"I'm sorry. We're going as fast as we can."

Boudreau's mouth tightened. "Just keep going. I'll stay here, hold 'em back."

"We'll make it. Come on, Sandy." He helped her to her feet and put his arm around her again. He turned them toward Boudreau's house and started walking.

Just then a loud crack followed by a whizzing sound split the air.

"Down!" Boudreau whispered. He remained standing and held the double-barreled shotgun at hip height and fired two shots.

Another rifle shot split the air.

"Mon Dieu," he heard Boudreau mutter. "I let them get too close."

Tristan pushed Sandy down behind a bush. He crouched beside her, listening. From what he could tell from the direction of the gunfire, the men were below his friend on the path, so any shot he took might hit Boudreau.

Within a minute, the men pursuing them loosed a barrage of gunfire. Boudreau threw himself to the ground.

"Boudreau," he called out quietly between rifle shots. "You okay?"

The Cajun waved his hand. His message was *I'm fine.* The fact that he used their sign language sent its own message. *Quiet! They're very close.*

More gunfire erupted from below them. Tristan ducked.

"Sandy?" He looked down at her, but she had her eyes closed. The corners of her mouth were white and pinched.

At that instant Boudreau rose, fired two thunderous rounds, ducked to reload in record time, then rose and fired two more rounds. He half turned and gestured to Tristan to head on to the cabin.

Tristan rose carefully. His leg was practically useless now. He felt as though he were dragging it. "San? Can you stand?"

She nodded. As they rose, two more shots rang out and Boudreau fired back.

He held out his hand for Sandy. She jerked and uttered a small, strangled moan as she straightened.

"I'm sorry, hon. I swear it won't be much longer. Just keep going for me. Can you?" He had no idea where his determination was coming from.

If he were alone, he was sure he'd have collapsed long ago and done the best he could until a bullet took him out. But he wasn't alone, so he couldn't give up. He wouldn't do that. Not to Boudreau, who'd saved his life at least twice already, and certainly not to Sandy and their baby. He had to keep going for them.

"Okay," she said breathlessly.

They set out again for the cabin, trusting Boudreau to fend off their attackers.

Chapter Twelve

By the time they saw Boudreau's cabin, every step for Tristan was a separate, blazing agony and a fool's bet on a losing hand. Odds were that his next step could send him sprawling.

The only reason he hadn't collapsed already was because he'd known Sandy couldn't make it on her own. Her breathing was so shallow that she was panting. For some reason, she wasn't recovering from the smoke as quickly as he was. His cough was almost gone and he was breathing more easily.

He stumbled through the cabin door and finally let go of Sandy. She flopped down onto the bed Boudreau had made for him. "Breathe deeply," he said. "Sandy. Listen to me."

She had her eyes closed, but she obediently tried to pull in a deep lungful of air, but it set off a coughing fit.

Boudreau came in on their heels.

"Miss Sandy," he said. "You got to breathe deep. Got to get all that smoke out of your lungs. Drink water, too. Get rid of the toxins the smoke make."

He pressed his fist into the middle of his chest. "Tristan, press on her diaphragm, gently, like this. Not hard. Just enough to make her blow as much air out of

her lungs as possible. Then let go. She'll have to breathe."
As he talked, Boudreau grabbed a hunting vest from a
nail behind the door.

Tristan nodded. "Got it," he said, pulling the handgun
from the vest. "Wait. Are you headed back out? Can't
you rest?"

But Boudreau shook his head as he stuffed the pockets
of the vest with shotgun shells. "Got to keep an eye out
for them. Can't let them get any closer. Long as we can
hold them off, we're okay. They got the path from here
to the dock blocked. We can't get down and anybody that
comes up this way's got to go through them."

"What about the north side, by the artesian spring?
Zach and I climbed up that way when we were kids."

Boudreau nodded. "When you weighed less than half
what you weigh now. Remember all that rain back a couple months ago, right before you were shoved off the
rig? It washed a gully across down below the spring.
Weren't really possible to go that way before, the spring
had eroded it so much. Now there ain't no way anybody
can get through there. It's like a gumbo mud moat around
my house."

"So they can't get to us without us seeing them on the
path, but we can't get out, either," Tristan said.

Boudreau sighed. "Let me get out there. I got to do
some thinking about what we need to do."

"Boudreau," Tristan said as his friend headed back
outside. "Be careful."

He was barely out the door when Sandy started coughing again and Tristan kept pressing on her chest.

"Oh," she said, gasping. "You're pushing all…the air
out. I can't…breathe."

"I've got to. You've inhaled a lot of smoke. I'll get you

some water." He didn't like how she looked at all. She was pale and her hands were trembling, as were her lips. She sat, limp, with her eyes closed.

From a bucket that sat on a wooden table, Tristan filled a cup with water and brought it to her. "Here. It's water. Take it." He lifted her right hand and pressed the cup into it.

She curled her fingers around it and lifted it to her lips.

He went back to the table and washed his hands, then brought a bowl of clean water over to the bed.

She had drunk about half the water. "That's good, hon, but you need to drink it all."

"I'm fine," she said, but talking made her cough again. She took another sip from the cup.

"Good. Now see if you can breathe deep on your own. You're doing better. We're going to get those lungs cleaned out."

He wrung out a wet cloth and started cleaning her face as she sipped water from the cup.

Then by the time he got her face clean, she started coughing again. She gasped and grimaced.

"Your throat hurting?"

She shook her head. "My tummy."

Tristan emptied the bowl and wrung out the cloth. "Like a stomach cramp?"

She shook her head and looked at him without blinking. "No. It *hurts*. I think something's wrong."

Tristan stopped wiping at a smudge on her cheek and studied her. "What do you mean? With the baby?"

She shook her head. "I don't know." She lifted her shirt above the waist of her jeans and placed her hand on the top of her baby bump. Beneath her fingers, the denim was dark and damp. Too dark.

Blood? His heart thudded against his chest as a sick fear overtook him. Dear God, was she losing the baby?

"Ugh. My jeans are wet." She looked at her hand, which was streaked with blood. "Tristan? Is that blood?" she said, her face turning pale.

"Yeah, there's a little blood," he said matter-of-factly, doing his best to mask his fear. "Do you remember running into anything?"

"I—I'm not sure. Tristan? What is it?"

"Don't worry, San, it's okay," he said, hoping it was. But what could have happened to make her bleed, except… "Lie back. I need to take a look."

Sandy took hold of his hand and pulled herself around so she could lie down. He pushed her shirt up again and immediately saw why she was bleeding.

There was a small hole in the jeans, about two inches to the right of the zipper.

"Oh, God," he whispered. He touched the ragged hole. There was no doubt what it was. It was a bullet hole. She'd been shot.

"Tris? What's wrong?" Sandy asked.

He tried to speak, but his throat had closed up and nothing, not even a squeak of air, could get through. He swallowed and tried again. "Damn jeans are *tight*!" he muttered.

"The little bean is getting bigger," Sandy murmured.

By the time Tristan got her jeans down and off over her feet there was a lot of blood. The tight jeans had apparently served as a compress, keeping the bleeding to a minimum.

Without their pressure, she was bleeding freely—too freely from the small entrance wound. He used a clean cloth to wipe the blood away from her rounded tummy so he could see the wound. It was no bigger than the hole in her jeans, but that was no comfort. She'd been shot—in her tummy—where she was carrying their baby.

He wanted to scream, but he couldn't. She was watching him with wide, frightened eyes, waiting for him to assure her that everything was all right. He had to hold it together for her, because for some reason she still thought he was strong.

"Okay," he said, doing his damnedest to keep his voice steady. "Looks like one of those bullets that were flying around hit you in the tummy, but it's not nearly as bad as all the blood makes it look."

"Bullet?" She lifted her head to try to see. "I was shot? Tristan?" She took one look at his face and started crying. "What about the baby?"

"Shh, everything's going to be okay," he said, hoping she would believe him. "Do you know when it happened?"

"No," she said, her eyes closed and her arms limp at her sides again. "When we stood up from behind that second bush, I thought the jeans zipper pinched me. Maybe it wasn't the zipper. Maybe it was a bullet."

It had to be. There had been a couple of shots fired about the time Boudreau had yelled at them to run.

"Tristan," she cried, grabbing his arm. "What about the baby!"

"Hey. I'm right here. I promise you, he's going to be fine." He mentally crossed himself and asked forgiveness for whatever kind of lie it was that spared a terrified, wounded young woman a horrible possibility.

"How can you know? You can't know. Bean!" she shrieked, wrapping her hands around her baby bump.

"Little bean?" Those two words were so low he barely heard them.

Boudreau appeared at the door. "Tristan, she's got to stay quiet." He looked at her belly. "Oh." He muttered a French curse word and propped his shotgun against the door facing.

Tristan met his gaze and saw the worry on his face. "Is there an exit wound?" he asked.

"I don't know," Tristan said. "I don't think so."

Boudreau's brows drew down. "Move over," he ordered.

Tristan moved.

Boudreau sat in his place. "Miss Sandy, I've got to look at your back for a minute. Okay? I'm going to lift you up. I hope it don't hurt too much. But I've got to do it. Okay?"

Sandy's eyes lifted to Tristan's, and he nodded. So she nodded at Boudreau.

He lifted her with his big hands and turned her toward him, onto her side. She sucked in a quick breath when he lifted her, but then she was quiet.

Boudreau examined her from her buttocks all the way up to her hairline. Then he looked at Tristan and shook his head.

Tristan felt a combination of relief and dismay. Relief that the bullet hadn't exited her body, leaving a much larger and more damaging wound than the entrance one.

But no exit wound could be worse. That meant that the bullet was still inside her. And if it had bounced off a bone, a bullet could do immeasurable damage to internal organs. The fog in Tristan's brain turned to a sharp, sheer panic.

That bullet was in there, inside his wife. She could be

hemorrhaging internally. If it had ripped into the womb, it could have hit the baby.

"Tris? What is it? Is it bad?" Sandy asked, her voice rising in pitch again. Tristan needed to say something comforting to her. He tried. But his voice wouldn't work.

His gaze met Boudreau's and he read the message in the old man's eyes loud and clear. *Do not upset your little wife.*

Substituting determination for truth, he turned to his wife. "No. Luckily your back's not bleeding, and that's a good thing," he said with a small smile.

Boudreau stood. "I got to go. I think they're pretty close. Can't give them a minute or they might be on top of us."

Tristan could see that Boudreau was past exhaustion. In his tired eyes and in the droop of his sinewy shoulders, Tristan could count how many hours it had been since he'd slept.

He looked back at Sandy and found her watching him with that same wide-eyed, frightened expression on her face.

"Are you still hurting?" he asked.

She nodded without taking her eyes off him.

Boudreau pointed to a box sitting on the rough-hewn table under the window. "There's salve and potion in there. The same potion I gave you. Don't give her much. And look in that trunk at the end of my bed. You might find a nightshirt she can wear. Tie a couple of cloths together to make a bandage to wrap around the wound. Miss Sandy, you hold pressure with your hand until he gets the cloth wrapped around. Okay?"

Her head moved infinitesimally.

Boudreau went back outside.

When Tristan brought the potion to Sandy with a chaser of water, she asked him, "Is it safe for the baby?" she asked.

Tristan nodded as he poured some of the milky liquid from the brown jug into a tin cup. "Boudreau wouldn't give it to you if it wasn't okay. But it'll probably make you sleepy," he said, brushing her hair back from her face again. "That's okay. Just go ahead and take a nap. I'll get you a nightshirt in a little while. Okay?"

"Tris?" she said softly. "I haven't felt him kick." Her eyes were shining with tears. "And I know that's a bad sign."

He smiled at her and touched her lips with his fingers. "No worries, okay? That baby's fine. He's tired, just like the rest of us." He touched her chin and leaned down and gave her a quick kiss on the corner of her mouth, but she didn't smile back at him. She closed her eyes and a lone tear slid down her cheek.

"I'm going to see what it looks like outside. I'll be close by," he said, then stood and stepped outside.

The first thing he saw in the dark sky was the fire. The yellow and orange flames licked at the sky. It was obviously out of control. The house had been his father's and his grandfather's before that. Now it and everything inside it was gone.

"Our friends do that?" he asked Boudreau.

"Yep," Boudreau said, walking up to stand beside him. "I'm pretty sure they used gasoline."

"It's going to burn to the ground."

"Yep."

Tristan watched the fire for a moment, then realized that besides the flickering light of the fire he saw red blinking lights.

"Fire trucks," he muttered. "They finally saw the smoke and fire from town. We didn't call them and God knows we don't have any neighbors out here."

Boudreau nodded. "I think that blue light's the sheriff. Reckon the fire department notified him."

"He'll be looking for us—well, Sandy and you."

"And he'll see the spent shells and the shot-out tires."

"Think he'll try to find you?"

"Wouldn't be surprised," Boudreau said, "but he can't do any good coming up here by himself. Sure do hope he'll call in the Coast Guard or some help from up in Houma."

Tristan understood what Boudreau was saying. If the sheriff tried to take the path to Boudreau's house, the assassins could pick him off like a trapped rabbit.

Boudreau shifted and lifted his head, as if he'd heard something. "Now, son, listen to me," he said quietly. "There's a crate buried in the ground in back. It's under the woodpile. Move the three logs on the far left, then pry the top off the crate. Inside there's another flare gun, more ammunition and a few small mines."

"Mines?" Tristan echoed. "You mean land mines? Where did you get mines?"

"Army surplus," Boudreau answered coolly, letting Tristan know by his tone that he wasn't referring to the neighborhood store that sold camouflage clothing and old ammo boxes. We're going to need some leverage to stay ahead of them, so I need you to pull out three of those mines for me, grab a bucketful of shells and load a flare gun. I'll be back to pick them up. I need it inside, ready to go, because I might not have much time."

After another few seconds of silence, Tristan said, "Boudreau, she hasn't felt the baby kick."

Boudreau didn't move, but his head bowed a fraction of an inch. "Can't do a thing but wait, son. A woman's body is a powerful thing when it's protecting a child. Have faith."

But Tristan heard a worried tone in the other man's voice. "What's the matter?" he asked.

"There's two of them varmints, at least. Maybe three. I don't know where they are. Like I said, I heard something a while back. Could have been them, but they never showed themselves, neither did they shoot."

"Two? Maybe three? You mean including the two you shot at the house? Because I only saw three total."

"Nope. Remember, I saw another guy get out of their truck. And there could have been another one still. I thought I saw a shadow, but I was intent on aiming at the one I did see, not checking shadows."

"Are you sure they're still following you? Maybe they turned back, or—" He'd almost said, *Or went another way*, but Boudreau had already told him there was only one way out. They were surrounded by swamp water that covered gumbo mud.

"They ain't turning around," Boudreau said. "Not with the firefighters and the sheriff down there. And if the sheriff tries to pursue them up here, he'll be like a sitting duck on that path."

"So they're lying in wait on the path for us to go down or the sheriff to come up."

"I suspect that's right. They might not have sense enough to know what the land around here is like, but I'll bet either them or their boss know how to read a topo map. He won't know about the log bridges to the hideout, though. All he can see on those maps is swampland."

Tristan nodded. For the first time in his life he found

himself hating the gumbo mud and murky waters of the bayou. Right now they weren't beautiful and mysterious— they were the reason he couldn't get Sandy to a doctor.

"God, Boudreau. We shouldn't have come up here. We're stranded now. We should have run for the car."

"I told you earlier, son. They shot your tires out."

"Then we should have—hell, I don't know—grabbed one of their trucks or run up the road toward town or called the sheriff. Something other than coming here to be trapped. Boudreau, she could die."

"Keep your voice down."

"Maybe we should go to the hideout." But as soon as Tristan said it, he knew he couldn't do it. He cursed. "I can't walk the log bridges. They were slippery and wobbly back when I was a kid, and this damn leg's already quitting on me."

Boudreau sent him a sidelong glance. "Then you'll crawl across if you want to live—and save your wife and that baby."

Tristan took a deep breath. Boudreau was right. He was acting like a spoiled kid. He straightened and looked Boudreau full in the eye. "Then I'll crawl across."

"Okay, then. Get her up and go. It's going to be dawn in a couple of hours and those varmints will probably think they can do things in the daylight they can't in the dark."

"You can't stay here by yourself. You're exhausted, too. I'll take her, then I'll come back."

"Nope. No, you won't, son. You come back here and I'll feed you to 'em and leave that bad leg for last, just so it'll hurt you longer."

"Yes, sir," Tristan said, too tired and worried to react to Boudreau's attempt at humor. "But what about the sheriff? What do you think is going to happen when he comes upon those guys? He'll figure they set the fire."

"Maybe," Boudreau said. "But he's not going to be expecting hostiles. If he tries to walk over here, he'll be thinking he'll see me and maybe your little wife. And that's all."

"We can't let them kill him."

Boudreau laid his hand on Tristan's arm. "Son, if you can think of something we can do, I swear I'll do it. But it's up to you. I'm all out of ideas. The only thing I got left is hide till they find us and try to pick them off, wait for the sheriff to bring in reinforcements, or attack them, although I'd rather not risk that. I don't know."

Tristan stared at him. For his entire life he'd looked up to Boudreau. He'd thought the old Cajun was the smartest man he'd ever known. He'd never heard him say the words *I don't know.*

In the silence, a bird sang out. Boudreau lifted his head, then he lifted his rifle. "Mockingbirds don't sing at night. That's them. Why don't you get inside there and find your little wife something to wear while I make sure those varmints aren't getting any closer."

Tristan fetched the mines and flares and brought them inside, along with some nylon rope he found back there. He pushed them underneath Boudreau's bed, then went to the old trunk. When he opened it and dug beneath the winter coat and a couple of blankets, he found something that surprised him. It was a gown. Not a nightshirt. A woman's nightgown, made of cotton with a lace collar.

He hesitated a second, then decided that Boudreau meant for him to find it and use it. But even as he tried to imagine the woman who had worn it here in this cabin, he vowed that if Boudreau didn't bring it up he never would.

He set the gown on the bed and fetched some rags, which he tore into long strips then tied together. He hated to wake her. She was sleeping peacefully. Her breathing was almost normal and she wasn't coughing every few breaths.

She woke up with little effort and he got the bandages around her and anchored the cloth without too much trouble. She was obedient and raised her arms so he could slip the gown over her head and down.

He wanted to hold her and kiss her and tell her how much he loved her, but there was no time for that. Sadly, there might never be if he didn't hurry up.

"Everything okay?" he asked as he pushed her gently down to sit on the bed so he could slip her shoes on.

Then he took her hands and urged her to stand. She did, leaning against him, the heat of her body reaching him through the gown and his shirt. Her cheek against the side of his neck felt hot. For a brief moment, he stood there, letting her heat warm him.

But then it occurred to him that she might be too hot. He put his palm against her forehead, but he couldn't decide if she was giving off the comforting yet sexy warmth of sleep or if she had a fever.

"Is it far?" she asked, her head lolling a bit. "I need to go back to sleep."

"It's not far, I promise," he said, squeezing her tight and kissing the top of her head. "Okay, hon, ready?" He guided her and supported her on his left side while he used a walking stick that Boudreau kept by the cabin door to steady his right side.

When they came out of the cabin, he didn't see Boudreau, but he wasn't worried. There hadn't been any gunfire and he knew if Boudreau felt he needed to know where he was, he'd have told him.

"Okay, Sandy. We're off," he said with more spirit in his voice than was in his heart. He didn't know how much longer his leg was going to work. He knew that for the sake of avoiding damage, he should have stopped hours ago. But that was under normal circumstances, when he was not trying to save his wife and unborn child.

He looked in the direction of the hideout. There was no path visible. In fact, there was no indication that there was anything but dense, thick groves of cypress and mangrove along the entire perimeter of Boudreau's little clearing. But he knew there was a narrow strip of dry land there somewhere. Not exactly a path, but a way to get to Boudreau's hideout. He just had to find it.

He'd been to the hideout several times in the past— twenty years before. Praying for enough sense to find the hideout and enough strength to get that far, he trudged on, supporting Sandy.

"Tris," Sandy said, her voice slurred. "Where we going?"

"We're going to have a spend-the-night party in Boudreau's hideout."

"Spend-the-night party?"

"Yep. At his hideout. It's a great place to play cowboys and outlaws. And it's comfortable, too. Like camping out."

"Tris? Don't patronize me," she said, her voice still soft and sleepy-sounding, but her tone was imperious. Tristan's heart ached at the familiar warning tone in her voice. She was still weighted down by the fog of sleep. If she were fully awake this would be the beginning of an all-too-familiar argument. So familiar that he could quote it. It would be a lot like the last argument they'd had.

"Why won't you tell me the truth? I've got sense enough to know that there's something wrong."

"I am telling you the truth. I do enjoy working on the rig. I like the computer work."

"I see you, Tristan. Every time you come home, you're more worried. You don't talk to me. You don't touch me."

"I'm talking to you right now."

"No. This is not you. You've changed. This person standing in front of me is not the man I've loved all my life."

"Well, I don't know who you think I am, but I can assure you, I'm me."

"See, this is what I mean. I just can't talk to you."

"Sorry," he said to his sleepy wife. "I didn't mean to patronize you. We're going to Boudreau's hideout for a day or two."

"Because of those men who set fire to the house?"

So she was awake enough to remember the fire. He felt her straighten. "They're looking for us, but they won't find us there."

"How long till we get there?"

"Not long. Just a few minutes more. I know you're sleepy."

She put her free hand on her baby bump. "My tummy hurts. Little bean, what are you doing to me?" she said, then stumbled a bit.

"Whoa," Tristan said, struggling to keep his balance and hold on to her at the same time. He shuddered as pain shot through his calf. "I know you're hurting. But you've got to be aware of everything, okay? We're going to have to walk over a log bridge, and every step counts. Try to wake up."

He hoped she wasn't bleeding again. He had no idea if there were bandages in the hideout. Knowing Boudreau, there probably were. He hoped his friend had stashed some medication there, too.

"Bridge?" Sandy roused a bit. "Not those log bridges you and Zach used to play on? They were so slippery."

"We'll be fine. The logs are sturdy. And they'll keep us from having to walk in the swamp water. It's not deep, but you know how the mud is, and there could be snakes or alligators. And besides, these are the only clothes we have, so we've got to stay dry and that means no matter how tired we are or how much we hurt, we've got to stay on the bridge."

"You'll be right beside me, won't you?"

Dismay and fear roiled through him. Would he make it better or worse for her if he walked with her across the narrow logs Boudreau had put between the tiny islands of dry land deep in the swamp? "I will. I'll be right beside you. I'm sorry your tummy hurts, but it'll be all right. It's just the bean, jumping around."

"Jumping bean," she said sleepily. Tristan's eyes stung and his throat wanted to close up. He had no idea what kind of damage the bullet had done to her or to the baby. If she was bleeding internally, he didn't know if she would live long enough to have the baby or if the baby was even alive.

What he did know was that it was his fault she'd been shot. He hadn't taken good enough care of her. He should have been between her and the shooters the entire time.

She was looking at him with a frown on her face. He started to say something, but she spoke first. "Don't worry, Tris. I'll be fine. You always take good care of me. I know I'm safe with you."

He nodded at her, then put his arm around her so she couldn't look up into his face. He shook his head disgustedly. She thought she'd be safe with him. Well, he'd made a major mess out of that. Not only had he abandoned her for two months, as soon as he came back to her, he'd brought nothing but trouble following in his wake.

Sandy's left hand rested on her baby bump, her fingers curled as if she was afraid to let go. He wanted to ask her if the baby had moved, but he was sure that if the bean had kicked or wiggled, she'd have told him. What if their child was dead?

"What's the matter, Tris? You got a cold? You're sniffing so much."

"Yeah, hon," he said, gritting his teeth and blinking against the wetness in his eyes. "I must have caught a cold."

Chapter Thirteen

It was a slow and pain-filled walk to the first log bridge, during which Tristan heard several faint rounds of gunfire that he couldn't identify. He thought he heard rifles and Boudreau's shotgun and a third, different sound that might have been the echo of the flare gun. It was hard to tell, what with the distance and the muffling effect of the trees and underbrush.

About the time Tristan thought that sawing his leg off with a nail file couldn't hurt any worse than continuing to walk on it, he came upon a familiar and welcome sight. It was a large pile of dried foliage, vines, branches, twigs and leaves.

It looked as though a small whirlwind had blown it into the shade of a big cypress tree. But Tristan could see Boudreau's hand in the carefully disarranged pile. He knew the back of the deceptive pile of underbrush and leaves was woven together to create a mat that fit over the opening to the hideout. The other three sides were a wall built of mud and vines and brush that had been there for who knew how many years and completely hid the rough-hewn lean-to from even the most suspicious eyes.

He pushed aside the cover of woven vines and branches. The inside was as clean and carefully maintained as it had always been. For a marginal shelter, it contained some surprising and clever amenities.

The lean-to was made out of scrap lumber and sturdy branches with a tarp draped over them. Over the years the wood had weathered and rotted and been replaced, as had the tarp. So the inside walls were an abstract patchwork of blue, silver and brown.

The largest item inside was a long, shallow wooden crate turned on its side. It was deep and wide enough to sleep one person easily or two if they were very close. The way it was positioned, it was always dry. The floor of the shelter was covered with thick sisal mats. They wicked water easily and kept the shelter floor feeling relatively dry.

Tristan got Sandy inside and laid her down in the makeshift bed. He found two thin wool blankets wrapped in plastic and took them outside to shake them. They looked clean and whole and the plastic hadn't been chewed through. So he covered Sandy with them. By the time he got her tucked in, he was shivering with exhaustion.

"I'm sorry, Tris," she murmured as she pulled the covers up to her chin. "You need to rest, too."

He shook his head. He didn't have the strength to answer her or tell her that she had nothing—*nothing*—to apologize for.

"What's in all the boxes?" Sandy asked, pushing a wad of blanket under her head as a makeshift pillow.

Tristan shot her a sidelong glance. "I thought you'd gone to sleep. You need to conserve your energy."

Sandy looked at her husband. The small scar on the side of his head where the roughneck's bullet had grazed him stood out against his dark hair. He sat with his back against the lean-to wall and his right leg carefully extended. He leaned his head back and closed his eyes.

"You're the one who needs to rest," she said. "You look like you're about to pass out. I haven't been up for two days."

"Actually, I don't think you've had much more sleep than I have," he said without moving.

"Well, I'm not down to one leg to walk on."

"No. You've just—" He stopped, but she knew what he'd been about to say. *You've just been shot in the stomach.*

He grimaced. "I'm going to watch for Boudreau."

"You are a stubborn, stubborn man," she muttered, then louder, she said, "I'm exhausted, but I'm not sleepy. What's Boudreau got in here?"

His shoulders rose a little, then relaxed. "Survival stuff. Canned food, coffee, water and tools like a can opener, a screwdriver, hammer. You know. Things you might need in an emergency."

"So this is a storm shelter?"

"Storm house, hideout, maybe even guesthouse."

"What?" Sandy lifted her head and stared at his profile. He grinned and her heart skipped a beat. She loved him so much. On the heels of that thought came the memory of her mother's words. *Don't fall in love if you can help it. By the time it's over, he'll own every tiny sliver of your broken heart.* Sandy smiled sadly, her gaze still on her husband. "Every sliver," she whispered.

"Hmm?" Tristan asked.

"Provisions and some tools? Is that all? This looks like a lot of crates."

"He's probably got some clothes in here. Maybe a couple of sleeping bags. He had one he'd let Zach and me use."

"That's what's in these big ones?"

"No. Actually that's his weapons stockpile."

"Weapons?" She wasn't sure if she liked sleeping in a weapons stockpile. "Not loaded, I hope. What kind?"

He sat up and wiped his face, rubbing his eyes wearily. "I remember a revolver and a few boxes of ammunition. Oh, and a gun-cleaning kit."

"A revolver. That's like a six-gun, isn't it?"

He nodded. "Maybe some shotgun shells, too, for his big gun."

"What about the other big crate?"

He shrugged. "I don't know. Boudreau caught me looking in that first one and nearly skinned my hide."

"Really? When was that?"

"Years ago. I wasn't thirteen yet. Maybe not even twelve. He got madder than I've ever seen him. He said, 'You never touch those crates. *Mais non.* You do not come here without me from now on. Understand, you?'"

Sandy chuckled softly. "You do a pretty good impression of him. Wow…" Her voice trailed off. After several seconds, she spoke again. "Tris?"

"Yeah, hon?"

"Are we going to be okay?"

He scooted closer to her and leaned over and kissed her on the temple. "We're going to be fine. The sheriff has to know that these guys are up here. He's probably got the Coast Guard on their way in helicopters, or at least standing by." Tristan had little hope that his words were true. He prayed that Sandy, who knew him so well, didn't notice.

"How long will they take?" she murmured, almost forgetting what she was asking about.

"Not long," Tristan whispered.

She yawned. "Probably going…sleep now."

Tristan sat down and carefully stretched out his legs. He hadn't meant for her to know how badly he was doing. But she knew him too well.

He stretched, trying to get the aches and knots out of his arms and neck. Everything hurt and quivered with fatigue. His calf muscle was on the verge of a cramp and so he flexed his foot, but his effort was too little too late. In spite of his care, the overworked muscle seized.

He clenched his jaw and massaged it, holding his breath against the pain. He tried to keep quiet, but once in a while a quiet moan or grunt would escape. Luckily, they didn't wake Sandy, who was snoring softly by the time the muscle settled down.

Watching her sleep was relaxing to him and he began to get drowsy. With a quiet curse, he straightened, stretched and looked at his watch. It was ten minutes after three. The sky was clear, but with the thick overhang of branches in this dense part of the swamp, there were lots of shadowy places. The sun wouldn't go down until after seven o'clock, but the bayou would be dark long before that.

He was worried about Boudreau. Tristan had been able to sleep a few hours, but his friend had been awake for as long, if not longer, than he had. He wasn't even sure if Boudreau had taken a nap in all that time.

It was frustrating to sit and do nothing, knowing Boudreau was out there, exhausted and sleep-deprived, defending them all alone. Still, it was Tristan's job to protect Sandy. And Boudreau knew the bayou better than anyone.

He shifted and felt something in his pocket. He pulled out the small rhinestone-encrusted baseball glove that hid a flash drive. He smiled as he turned it in his hand. He'd chosen the baseball glove on a whim, hoping it might portend a boy. The fact that it matched the mobile closely enough that he could hide it in plain sight was a happy accident.

Thank goodness he'd grabbed it. The tiny, sparkly flash drive held the recordings that he hoped would match Vernon Lee's voice. He wanted to see the evil man's multibillion-dollar empire fall.

A shot rang out and he jumped. The report sounded like a rifle, so it was one of Lee's men. He waited, listening for Boudreau to return fire with his shotgun, but heard nothing.

Boudreau must not want to give away his position by firing back. At least, Tristan hoped that was why he was quiet.

Still, just in case, Tristan crawled inside the lean-to and grabbed one of the large magazines for his handgun. He inserted the magazine, then hefted the gun to feel how the extra weight was distributed. Not bad. He positioned himself in the opening of the lean-to, where he could see and hear.

"Tris." Sandy's sleep-softened voice floated over him.

"Hey," he said. "Go back to sleep."

"What's going on?" she asked.

"It's okay. I heard something."

"A gunshot," she said matter-of-factly. "What's that blue thing you're holding? Is that part of the mobile over the baby's crib?"

He looked at it. "It's—" He was momentarily stumped. Did he tell her what it was and explain that this was the proof that Vernon Lee had tried to kill him? Or did he make up something?

"Wait. Shh. I think I hear something again."

She lifted herself up on one elbow. "No, you don't. What's the deal about the baseball glove?" She stared at it. "Oh, I see. It's a flash drive. That's your evidence, isn't it? You hid it in the nursery? In the mobile?"

Tristan let it dangle from his fingers. "I was going to transfer the files to Homeland Security the next time I was home," he said quietly.

"But you never came home," she said, her voice breaking. "You should have told me. I could have sent it to Maddy."

He nodded. "I thought there was time. I won't make that mistake again,"

Her eyes filled with tears. "I won't, either," she said.

Tristan looked away. He was afraid if their gazes held very long Sandy would see the worry in his eyes.

"Tris?"

He winced at her tone. "Sandy—"

"No, wait. What's going to happen? It looks to me like there's a standoff. I'm afraid two injured people and one exhausted man are no match for those men."

He had a reassuring answer all planned, but a noise interrupted him. He held up a hand.

"Shh!" he said.

He heard the sound of footsteps tromping through the woods toward them. He slid inside the lean-to and pulled the cover across in front of him, leaving a small slit. Carefully, he thumbed the toggle switch on the side of the weapon to Auto.

When Boudreau appeared from the tangled woods,

relief cascaded through Tristan's veins. His friend was all right.

The first thing the Cajun said was "Cover's not all the way over the opening."

"I left myself room to see and shoot. Sandy was asleep on her feet, so I got her tucked in as quickly as I could," Tristan said defensively, knowing that wasn't the whole truth. He was too tired and so he was making mistakes and Boudreau knew it.

"Going too fast can slow you down a lot, yeah," Boudreau said as he looked around 360 degrees, then stared at nothing, listening.

While Boudreau checked out the area, Tristan checked him out. His sun-browned face had a greenish-gray tint to it, and his mouth was drawn down and pinched looking. His eyes looked weak and his shoulders were slumped even more than they'd been a couple of hours ago at the cabin. "You're about dead on your feet. Climb in there and take a nap. I'll keep watch."

"*Non.* Something to eat and some water and I'll be fine."

Tristan reached back into the lean-to and pulled out one of the small food crates.

Boudreau pried the wooden lid open with the big knife he always carried. There were two glass jugs inside and what looked like jerky and some kind of fruit and nut bars in a glass jar. Boudreau grabbed a jug and drank about a pint of liquid out of it.

"That's water?" Tristan asked.

Boudreau nodded and handed the jug to Tristan, who took a long drink, then stuck his head inside. "San? Want some water?"

She opened her eyes to a small slit. "Please," she said. Tristan left the bottle with her.

Boudreau grabbed a handful of jerky and closed the glass jar. "She doing okay?" he asked softly.

"I don't know. I don't think she's bleeding anymore, but she felt hot. I think she has a fever."

"Could be," Boudreau said. "I reckon it's time to fight."

Tristan flung his head back and sighed deeply. "I guess we can hope they're as tired as we are."

"Probably are. Plus, although they got good weapons, they're slow and they don't know the swamp."

"They don't, but hell, Boudreau, you're so exhausted you probably can't lift your gun, and I'm not even half a man with this leg."

Boudreau lifted the shotgun to his shoulder and aimed at the path. "This look like I can't lift my gun?"

Tristan didn't bother answering his question. "How close are they?"

"Probably as close as they can get without running into the mines."

"The mines?" Tristan said, "What did you do? Are they going to step on them?"

"*Non.* I don't want to kill them. I want them to turn tail and run right smack into the sheriff. I chopped down all but one log on the longest bridge and I wired a mine in full view on either end of the log."

Tristan tried to picture what Boudreau was describing. Each mine was about fourteen inches in diameter. It might fit across the log. "Can't they jump over them or remove the wires?"

"Son, how long you known me? Did you ever see me do something halfway?" Boudreau didn't wait for Tristan to answer. "They can try to do something with the mines, but it wouldn't be a good idea. I wrapped the wire that I used to fasten 'em to the trigger. If they try to cut the wires or unwrap them they're liable to blow themselves up." He chewed on the jerky. "And the way I've got the wire strung, they can't jump high enough from that wobbly log over the mine without catching their feet on the wire. They should know they can't touch them. And if they try to walk through the swamp—"

"The gumbo mud'll get them." Tristan studied him. "Sounds like you covered every base."

Boudreau shrugged and bit off another piece of jerky. "Not every one." He paused for a beat. "There's one thing they could do. It's chancy, for them and us. It could work, but it could also—"

His words were interrupted by a huge explosion. Actually two explosions right on top of each other. Boudreau tossed the last bite of jerky down in disgust. "—blow up the log bridge," he finished. "Push that biggest crate out here."

Boudreau pried the lid off with his knife, then cursed in Cajun French. "I was counting on these grenades, but they're corroded."

"So they're duds?"

Boudreau shook his head. "*Non.* Worse than duds. Duds are dead. These, you don't know if they'll explode on time or if they'll go off in your hand before you can even pull the pin."

Tristan shuddered at that thought. Looking into the crate, he saw the white crystals that covered the grenades. "What should we do with them?" he asked.

"They been fine here for fifteen years. They'll probably stay fine, long as nobody bothers them."

"So if we don't have grenades, what are we going to use?"

Boudreau pushed himself to his feet, grunting at the effort. "Our heads, son. We're going to have to use our heads. Now let's go. We've got to disarm some bad guys. Let's hope they ain't too smart to get stuck in the mud."

SANDY HEARD PEOPLE TALKING, she thought. She couldn't be sure because her ears were ringing from the explosion that had shocked her out of a restless doze.

"Tristan?" Her voice echoed in her ears. She yawned, trying to get rid of the ringing.

Tristan stuck his head into the lean-to. "Hey," he said. "Did the explosion wake you?"

His voice was distorted, too. She rolled her eyes at him as she moved to get up. When she did, a sharp, stinging pain hit her stomach. Her hand flew to her tummy. "Oh!" she cried. "Oh, no!"

"What's wrong?" Tristan asked.

"I think I tore the cloth away from the wound." She looked up at him and felt tears start in her eyes. "I forgot," she muttered, wrapping her hands around her tummy protectively.

Tristan crawled over to sit beside her and pulled her close. "Let me see." He checked the bandage on her tummy. "I think you're okay. I don't feel or see any blood and the bandage is still in place."

She shook her head. "You don't understand. I wasn't careful. I went to sleep and forgot about the baby," she said, sniffling. "I forgot him. And not only that. I forgot I'd been shot. I forgot that he…he might not be okay." Now she was crying in earnest.

She pressed one hand to her heart and the other to the

spot on the right side of her tummy where the little bean liked to kick. "Oh, Tristan, I for…got—" She sobbed.

Tristan pulled her close and held her, his face pressed into her hair, his hand still on her baby bump. "It's not your fault. I gave you something to help you sleep. You probably were dreaming—"

"Stop." She laid her hand over his. "It's because he's not moving—" Her words were cut off by a sob.

"Wait," Tristan said. "Be still."

"What if he's—"

"Shh." He pressed harder.

Then she felt it and her fingers curled against the back of his hand. Had she really felt a tiny kick?

"San?" Tristan's voice was unsteady. "Did I just feel something?"

She looked down at her baby bump, then up at him. "He kicked," she murmured, almost overcome by relief.

"I know," he said, his voice unsteady with awe.

"He kicked! Oh, Tris, he's alive!"

"Tristan!" Boudreau's gruff voice called from outside the lean-to. "We got to go. Even an idiot can figure out how to move through the mud, if you give him enough time."

Tristan closed his eyes and sat still. She could feel the fine trembling of his hand against her skin, even through the bandage and the nightgown.

"Tristan!" Boudreau sounded irritated.

"Coming!" Tristan called, then he leaned over and kissed her. She was still crying, but now it was with joy. Her baby was alive. She kissed Tristan back, feeling the same thrill and the same growing flame that she felt every time, whether it was a kiss of passion during lovemaking or a sweet, tender kiss, like this one right now.

He pulled away reluctantly. "Got to go help Boudreau take care of those guys," he told her as he pulled a long, curved magazine and three normal ones from Boudreau's weapons crate.

Once he'd stored the ammunition in the hunting vest, he kissed her once more. "Stay here and stay hidden. You'll be fine. I'll be right back," he said.

Sandy knew he was lying. He and Boudreau were exhausted. Neither of them had the strength or stamina to stand up to the men chasing them.

She watched him as he crawled awkwardly out of the lean-to, wincing as every movement hurt his leg.

Despite her determination, the tears started again. "You lying liar," she whispered, too quietly for Tristan to hear. "You'd better come back. I don't want to lose you again."

Tristan pulled the camouflaged mat over the lean-to's opening while Boudreau talked about the best way to approach the log bridge. After a few minutes Sandy heard their footsteps crunching on the forest floor and fading as they got farther and farther away, until she could no longer hear anything.

She sat there for a few moments, willing him to turn around and come back, but knowing in her heart that he would never do that.

She'd felt betrayed and heartbroken when she'd found out he'd been recuperating less than a mile from their home. But now she understood that he hadn't left her alone. He had done everything he could to protect her.

"Bean, your daddy's crazy if he thinks I'm going to sit here and do nothing while he's in danger," she whispered. She looked around at the crates. Tristan hadn't known what was in most of them. They were worth exploring. She might find something that they could use.

"But first, we've got to find that revolver he mentioned. I don't know anything about guns, but I'll bet I can handle a six-shooter." She patted her tummy. "I heard them say there were at least two of those *varmints* out there, little bean. That gives me three shots each."

Chapter Fourteen

Boudreau was at least two hundred yards ahead of Tristan. Before he could catch up, rifle shots rang out. Tristan listened but didn't hear the bass roar of Boudreau's shotgun.

"Bastards," he muttered, doing his best to run. "You'd better not hurt him."

The first thing he saw as the tangle of vines, branches and brush began to thin were the two small craters left by the exploded mines. The craters were shallow, but the force of the blast had knocked the log that connected the two islands of dry land into the swamp.

The next thing he saw was a man hip deep in the swamp, holding a rifle up over his head with one hand and trying to grasp a wet, slippery cypress knee with the other.

Tristan knew exactly what had happened. The man had jumped in, fooled by the deceptively calm surface, figuring he could walk across the firm bottom and climb up onto the dry knoll on the other side.

Instead, he'd found himself ankle deep in what the folks in South Louisiana called gumbo mud. It stuck to everything—skin, boots, tires and itself.

The other man was on dry ground, on the knoll behind

his partner. He was yelling at his buddy to stop struggling, because he was only making things worse.

Tristan gave the man on dry ground a second look. He
was one of the kidnappers. The one who'd held a gun on
him and had tossed him across the pier.

Finally, Tristan spotted Boudreau. The Cajun was
crouched down behind a lantana bush. There was blood
staining the left sleeve of his shirt. A hollow dread
washed over Tristan. He'd never seen Boudreau hurt or
ill. His friend had always been invincible, larger than life.

It took all Tristan's willpower not to rush over to him.
Boudreau's head angled slightly in his direction, signal-
ing that he knew Tristan was there. Then he moved it
back and forth in a negative shake. Tristan read him loud
and clear.

Stay back. Let them dig their own graves.

He could live with that. Carefully and silently, he
shifted his weight to his left foot and got as comfortable as he could. He gripped the automatic handgun and
waited to see what the two men were going to do. As he
relaxed, the men's yelling began to coalesce into words
and phrases.

"Stop thrashing around!" the kidnapper yelled. "If
you fall over you'll never get up."

He was right. The more the man in the water struggled, the more the mud sucked him down.

"You got anything that might actually *help*, Echols?"
the man in the mud shouted.

"Maybe stand still and see what happens. And careful
with that rifle. I need you to be able to shoot."

Boudreau's head lifted about a quarter inch. Tristan
was barely a second behind him in realizing that the
man was beginning to figure out how to handle the mud.

Boudreau pushed himself up onto his knees and raised his shotgun. Tristan held his breath. Was he going to shoot one of them? That wasn't like him, but then Tristan wouldn't have thought it was like Boudreau to shoot the *Pleiades Seagull*'s captain without hesitation, either, for ordering Tristan killed.

"Bonjour, varmints," Boudreau said and shot the ground around three feet in front of Echols's feet. Echols jumped backward and nearly tripped. Boudreau emptied the second barrel two feet in front of his toes.

"What the hell?" Echols yelled and raised his rifle again.

"Why don't you explain what you doing chasing us?" Boudreau yelled. "'Cause I'm tired, me. I'm ready to go to the house."

"We want Tristan DuChaud. My boss wants to talk to him."

Tristan stepped far enough forward to be seen, but not so far that he couldn't take cover if either of the men started shooting.

"Hi there. Remember me?" he shouted.

The kidnapper Echols threw his hands out in a frustrated gesture. "You. Still cocky as ever."

"Oh, I'm not cocky," Tristan said. "Just confident. So how you been?"

"Tristan," Boudreau said. "Don't get too cocky."

Tristan felt his face grow warm. Boudreau was right. This was serious business. He had no business acting as though it was not. "Well, Echols, here I am. What's Vernon Lee got to say to me?" he asked, watching Echols closely, waiting to see his reaction to the name of the owner of Lee Drilling.

It was the man in the water who reacted. He tried to

lower his rifle to his shoulder, but the movement nearly toppled him into the water. Quickly he raised his arms again, waving them like a tightrope walker trying not to fall.

"How'd he figure out—"

"Shut up!" Echols yelled, then aimed his weapon at Tristan.

Tristan didn't react. He just kept his gaze on the man's hands and continued talking. "You're just going to shoot me? Here's an idea. Have your buddy record it on his phone so you can prove to Vernon Lee that I'm dead—this time.

"Oh, wait." Tristan gestured toward the man in the water. "He's sinking already. If he drops the phone, you'll have nothing. Legend says that the gumbo mud'll suck you all the way to the center of the earth."

"What?" the man in the mud screeched. "I'm sinking? How deep is this—" He looked down. "Echols? Get me out of here."

"Shut the hell up and throw that rifle over here."

"What? Oh, hell no!"

"Do it. We need that gun and without it, you can move much easier. Plus, if you drop it in the mud it'll be ruined."

Tristan saw Boudreau turn to look over his shoulder at him. "You okay?" Tristan called.

"Yeah. They just winged me."

"Look out!" Tristan cried suddenly as he saw Echols swing his rifle in Boudreau's direction. The Cajun dropped to the ground just as the rifle's loud crack split the air. The bullet tore through the brush above Boudreau's head. Then without hesitating, Echols whirled and fired off two rounds at Tristan.

Tristan hit the dirt where he stood as the bullets whistled by his ear. He waited a beat, then peered over the tangle of vines. Dappled sunlight glimmered off the steel barrel of the rifle as the man swung it back and forth between him and Boudreau, gauging how low to aim to send a bullet through the underbrush and directly into their bodies.

There was no time to check on Boudreau. Tristan lifted the automatic handgun and pressed the trigger. A burst of about six or eight shots spewed out of the gun, much faster than Tristan could count.

He dropped again at the very instant that his hand flew upward from the recoil. A squeal told him his wild volley had hit at least one man, probably the one in the mud. He doubted Echols was a squealer.

"I'm hit!" the man cried.

"Throw that gun over here before you drop it!" his partner yelled.

But the man stuck in the gumbo mud ignored him. He scooted sideways enough to steady himself against the cypress knee. He'd finally stopped struggling. There was blood on the left side of his shirt, but not much. The wound probably was a graze. As Tristan watched, he lifted the rifle and fired off a couple of wild rounds one-handed.

Then Echols joined the fray, and bullets spattered the leaves and branches all around Tristan. He had to stop them somehow. He didn't want to kill them, nor did he want Boudreau to have another death on his conscience, but what he wanted took a backseat to his determination to do whatever it took to get Sandy out of there and to a doctor.

"Tristan." Boudreau's voice was a little breathless.

"Get on back there. I'll take care of these two. You need to take care of yours."

Tristan fired again another volley. More rifle slugs bursting all around them. "You go," he called to Boudreau. "I'll take care of these guys. They can't have much more ammunition."

"Neither one of you are going anywhere," Echols said. Tristan rose up and took a look. Echols had been hit, too. Blood was staining the front of his shirt. But he had the rifle up and aimed again.

Then Tristan heard a sound that nearly stopped his heart. It was footsteps, treading lightly on the path behind him. There was only one person in the world it could be. He prayed he was wrong, even though he knew he wasn't.

"Sandy," he whispered through gritted teeth, when he heard the footsteps stop a few feet behind him. "Get the hell back to the hideout *now* or I swear to you I will shoot you myself."

"Tristan," Sandy whispered. "I found some grenades."

"What? Sandy!" Shock and gut-wrenching fear sent Tristan's pulse skyrocketing. "Damn it. Didn't you hear Boudreau? Those things are corroded and unstable. They could go off in your hands!" He shimmied backward until he was deep enough into the foliage that hopefully Echols couldn't see him. He pushed himself to his feet.

"Corroded? No, they're not. Look." She was holding a small metal box. She started to lift the lid.

"Where did you get that?" he demanded. He hadn't seen any metal containers in the lean-to.

"Inside a big crate. They were the only thing in there."

Behind them a rifle shot cracked, then another and another. "Get down!" he yelled. He grabbed her and pulled her down with him. She pushed the metal box into his hands. He opened it carefully. But instead of white crystals, he saw four perfectly good grenades, with shiny pins intact. "Boudreau," he called. "Metal box in the hideout? Can't be very old."

"Metal box?" Boudreau repeated. "Ooh-la-la. I put that in there the day before I pull you out of the water. I guarantee I plumb forgot."

Tristan kissed Sandy briefly. "I love you. Get back to the lean-to."

She glared at him. "I've got the revolver. I'm going to help."

"The hell you are."

"Tristan, you know what to do with those?" Boudreau called.

But Tristan didn't answer him. "You have to go back," he said to Sandy. "I mean it. You've probably saved our lives by finding these grenades. But I'm not letting you get shot again."

"I'm not going to sit in that lean-to and wait to see who shows up, you or them." The glare that Sandy aimed at him was nothing short of a laser, drilling straight into his heart. "I will never sit back and wait for you again, you stubborn lying liar."

He closed his eyes, hoping the stinging behind them would not turn into vision-blurring tears. "Sandy, I love you. I will never lie to you for your own good. I will never ever leave you. But please stay back. Please keep you and the little bean safe so I can get you both out of here."

She opened her mouth, then closed it. The laser glare dimmed as her mouth thinned grudgingly. "Fine. Okay. For the baby."

Tristan breathed a sigh of relief, then scooted back

to his shooting position. "Boudreau? We've got four," he said.

"Shh!" Boudreau whispered. "Listen."

Tristan froze, listening. Echols was talking. Not yelling. Talking. Tristan took a quick peek. "He's got a satellite phone," he whispered to Boudreau. "If we can get our hands on that, we can call the sheriff and he can get a position on us."

"We're stuck back in the swamp," Echols was saying. He hadn't even tried to lower his voice. The tiny knoll he was on wasn't big enough for him to have a private conversation. He knew that Tristan and Boudreau could hear every word. "In a standoff, facing each other on two islands surrounded by a sticky mud that sucks you down into it and won't let go. Farrell is stuck in it."

He stopped talking and listened. "You did! Yes, sir! Thank you, sir. I'll be listening for it. Tell them they can't land here. Not enough solid ground. They'll have to hover and send down a harness to pull us up."

He paused, listening. The relief on his face turned to terror. "But—but, Mr. Lee, you can't do that. We're right here, not fifty yards away. That won't work. The strafing will hit us, too. We've done our jobs, sir! Please. You have to get us out! Mr. Lee, no! Mr. Lee? Sir?"

Farrell, who had been listening, forgot what he'd learned in the past few moments and started struggling again. "Strafing? Oh, my God! That rat bastard Lee is going to kill us, isn't he? Damn it, Echols, I told you we'd never get out of this alive." He tried to pick up his right leg, then his left. "I can't move," he shouted. "Help me!"

Tristan's pulse was hammering again, this time because of what he'd heard. Both of the men had used the name Lee for the man who had just called them on the satellite phone and told them he wasn't going to rescue them. From Echols's side of the conversation, it sounded as if Lee was sending a helicopter. The bird could probably pinpoint their location from the satellite phone and Tristan had little doubt about its orders.

Lee apparently wanted no loose ends. So he'd ordered the helicopter to strafe the entire area, thereby killing Tristan, Boudreau and Sandy and Lee's own men in one pass of the helicopter.

"Hey, Echols," he called out. "Things don't sound good for you and your buddy there. What do you say we team up to stay alive? I'll help you if you'll help me. Call the sheriff on that phone. I'll give you his number."

Echols set the phone down and lifted his rifle. "Call the sheriff so he can shoot us or arrest us or try us for treason?"

"He won't shoot you, I'm pretty sure. And arrested for treason? It's better than being strafed alongside your enemy, right?"

Echols glared at him. "Why should I believe you'd even think about keeping your word?"

Tristan pushed himself to his feet and took another step out of the foliage. "Maybe you shouldn't. But I'll tell you this. I'm one of the good guys. I want to get out of here. My friend is wounded." They probably knew that Sandy was with him, but he wasn't going to mention her. "I'm no more interested in being strafed by Lee's helicopter than you are."

Echols stared at him for a long time.

A vague sound reached Tristan's ears. Farrell heard it at the same time Tristan did.

"Oh, my God!" he screamed. "That's a helicopter! For the love of heaven call the damn sheriff! I don't want to die here." He turned and tried to make his way to the knoll where his partner waited, but he slipped and sank to his armpits.

"Echols!" he yelled, in full panic mode now. "Call him, man! You've got kids, just like me."

"Call the sheriff," Tristan pleaded. "You know Lee's got a copter on the way. You've got to know the sheriff is searching for us, too. He mentioned the Coast Guard. We all heard the fire trucks. I'm sure the sheriff was right behind them."

"I'm sinking, Echols! Help me! Make the call!"

Echols made a shushing gesture, then asked Tristan, "How do I know you won't shoot me?"

Tristan shrugged. "You don't. But I haven't shot you yet and you and your buddy both are wide-open. Not to mention you could shoot me, too. Come on. You're trading certain death for a trial and a possible prison sentence."

"And if I decide to take my chances with my boss?"

"It's your funeral." Tristan shrugged. "Oh, wait a minute. I forgot to mention one thing. Lee won't have the pleasure of blowing you up after all." He reached into the box and grabbed one of the grenades. "See what I've got?" He held it up high so Echols couldn't help but see it.

"What the hell?"

"This? It's a good ol' US-military-grade grenade. You know what a grenade is, don't you?"

"You won't detonate that so close to you."

"That could be a smart bet, but the stakes are pretty high, I guarantee. We've got a lot more room over here. We can run. Besides, I can throw it way on the other side of you. Of course, if you call the sheriff for me, I won't have to waste these."

Echols was silent. Farrell talked almost the entire time, his tone varying from pleading to screeching to rationalizing.

Finally Echols switched the rifle to his left hand and picked up the satellite phone. "Give me the number."

"And one last little thing," Tristan said. "Thanks to you guys, the sheriff thinks I'm dead. You might have to do a little explaining to convince him that I'm alive."

"What? How am I supposed to explain that?"

"You could tell him about your boss, Vernon Lee."

Farrell was still pushing himself toward the knoll. He'd figured out that lifting each leg high enough and shaking it could help the water melt the sticky mud. It was excruciatingly slow, but it worked.

Tristan made a show of setting down the metal box of grenades and the automatic pistol. Empty-handed, he called out to Echols. "Come closer to the edge and hold the phone up so I can talk to him."

Echols started forward, but Tristan held up his hand. "First, drop your weapons. I did."

"Nope. I'm keeping my handgun," Echols said emphatically. "And I'm not talking to the sheriff. You can do your own explaining. You'll have to yell at the phone."

He could do that, but he did not really want to leave his cover and walk over to the edge of the dry land in order to be heard. That was probably stupid. Either of the men would have an easy shot.

"What are you doing?" his wife's voice whispered from behind him. "You can't go out there."

Tristan's heart jumped. "Damn it, Sandy. What are you doing here? I told you to go back to the hideout. I should have known you weren't going to listen to me. When have you ever?" He shook his head as he started forward.

"You know that this is the best chance we've got to get out of here. I've got to let the sheriff know that I'm alive. The only way he'll believe it is if he hears me himself."

"They will shoot you. Then they can call Lee and tell him you're dead and they'll be safe."

She was right. That was a possibility. But he'd heard Echols's voice on the phone. Echols knew that Lee was going to kill them. "It's a chance I've got to take," he told her, then looked at Echols. "Okay," he called to Echols. "I'll trust you."

"Tristan!" Sandy snapped. "That's like telling a hornet on your leg you'll trust him not to sting you while you're trying to get him off. So what if they trust you. You cannot trust them."

"Give me the number," Echols shouted.

Tristan gave him the number. He keyed it in and waited, the bulky phone held to his ear. Within a few seconds, his face changed from trepidation to a vague relief. But then how relieved could he feel about the certainty of being imprisoned for treason, kidnapping, assault with intent, arson and whatever else the government might want to charge him with. Of course, one difference was that when he faced a United States court, he could be relatively sure he'd come out alive. From how he'd responded to Vernon Lee earlier, it sounded as if Lee's plan was to wipe the slate clean. Get rid of not only Tristan, but the assassins he'd sent.

"Is this the sheriff?" Echols asked. Then he went on, "I'm calling regarding Tristan DuChaud." There was a long pause, then, "You don't need to know my name. Not yet. But I've got news for you. DuChaud is not dead." He listened for a moment, his gaze on Tristan.

"I'm standing here looking at him. Where? Hell, I don't know. Somewhere in the swamp."

The sheriff talked again and Echols looked at Tristan, frowning. "I don't know about his wife. She was in the house?"

Tristan shook his head.

"DuChaud is telling me she wasn't in the house." He listened, then sighed. "Yes. Fine. Fine. I set the fire. Yes, that was us, too. We shot at you when you tried to take the path to the dock." Echols listened some more, then looked at Tristan again. "He wants to talk to you."

"Sheriff!" Tristan shouted. "Can you hear me?"

"Hello?" the sheriff said. "I was about to hang up. Who the hell is this?"

"Sheriff Nehigh," Tristan yelled. "It's Tristan DuChaud."

"What? DuChaud's deceased. What's going on here? I warn you, I've got helicopters on the way. You guys are in big trouble and this is not funny. I'm having your phone traced."

"Barley," he yelled desperately, hoping that using the sheriff's nickname would convince him. "I'm Tristan DuChaud. You dated my sister in high school. We're on a satellite phone. I'm *not* dead. Boudreau, tell him."

Boudreau sat up and bellowed, "Sheriff, it's Boudreau here. Tristan tells the truth. He is alive."

"Boudreau? DuChaud?" Sheriff Nehigh said. "I just got word from the Coast Guard that their helicopters have picked up your signal. They'll be on top of you in no time." The sheriff cleared his throat. "Now, we got some time. Tell me this. What the hell is going on?"

Chapter Fifteen

When Sandy opened her eyes, everything was glowing an odd, ugly sea-green color. She blinked and looked around. It was a hospital room and she was in a hospital bed.

Her first thought was that she'd lost the baby and her pulse leaped in fear, but then he kicked.

"Ow, bean," she whispered. "That was a good one."

When she took a breath the harsh smell of antiseptic stung her nostrils and made her sneeze.

Sneezing made her hurt, deep in her stomach. She moaned a little, then lifted her head to look around. She wanted to shift her position, but when she tried to put her hands down on the mattress, she felt a pull and a small sting on the back of her right hand. IV solution. Bandage. Soreness.

On the wall in front of the bed was a whiteboard and a plastic box. It was too dim in the room to read what was written in green marker on the white board, but the box was labeled *Biohazard, Warning: Risk of Contamination* and *Dispose of Properly* in red letters.

Of course. She was in a hospital room.

She tried to remember how she got here, but her brain was hazy and the memories were more like dreams that always fluttered away on butterflies wings when she tried to catch them.

A vision of Tristan yelling across the swamp came to her. Was that the last thing she remembered?

She closed her eyes and explored her memory as well as she could. What had happened between that snippet of time and now was in there. She knew it was, if she could just access it.

Within seconds of closing her eyes, she began to drift off to sleep. While sleeping some more seemed like a great idea, she wanted to remember, so she flexed her right hand and the pain from the IV cannula stung her again, pushing away her drowsiness.

A memory of the prick of a needle and a voice promising that she'd relax soon came to her.

Well, she'd relaxed, all right. She could barely hold her eyes open. She glanced at her left wrist. Her watch was gone.

That made sense. They didn't let anyone wear jewelry into surgery.

Surgery? She'd had surgery? From somewhere came a faint recollection of a male voice telling her she wouldn't remember a thing, then lots of painfully bright lights hurting her eyes.

She wondered what time it was. She squinted at the clock on the wall above the whiteboard, but the green glow in the room was too dark to see the time.

Suddenly, she had to know the time. She felt along the edge of the hospital bed, looking for the buzzer. And she was thirsty.

When she turned her head as she felt for the buzzer, she was startled to see a figure in a chair beside the bed.

She pressed her left palm against her chest, where her heart pounded.

The sight of the shadowed figure triggered more memories, this time of endless questions.

Suddenly, it all came rushing back. The hammering interrogations had started with the EMTs on the helicopter and continued with the emergency-room staff downstairs.

But they were nothing compared to the grilling she'd gotten from the sheriff, a Homeland Security Agent, a member of the Governor of Louisiana's staff and a rather handsome, if uptight, young man who had never explained who he was.

And now here was *another* stranger, waiting for her to wake up? No. She pressed her lips together tightly.

"No," she muttered. "No more questions." Not until she got to ask a few of her own.

She reached for the buzzer again, so she could tell the nurse to get rid of this man, whoever he was, but she couldn't find its cord.

Suddenly tired, she laid her head back on the pillow. "Well?" she said, letting her eyes drift closed. "What do you want?"

The man didn't answer. She glanced sideways at him, then lifted her head to look more closely. He was sitting awkwardly, his head bowed.

He'd fallen asleep. She leaned as far to the left as she could and squinted, trying to make out his features in the early-morning sea-green light. As soon as her eyes focused on his face, her heart skipped a beat.

"Oh," she breathed. "Tristan."

He stirred and lifted his head.

She reached out to him.

"Hey, San," he murmured, reaching out to take her hand. "Are you all right? The nurses wouldn't tell me anything except that you were *resting comfortably*."

"Oh, Tris." Her voice broke. He was really here. "Oh, my Tristan."

And then her brain was awash with everything that had happened, from the fire to the running and hiding in the swamp to listening to the doctors talking about the miracle that was her baby.

The images and words rushed past her like fast-flowing river water. After a moment, she tried to verbalize some of it.

"I remember waking up in the ER and thought the past few days were a dream. I thought I was back in that world where you were dead."

He took her hand and wrapped his around it, then kissed her fingers. "I'm not dead," he whispered. "Feel this?" He pressed a trail of kisses onto her skin, from the back of her hand to her forearm to her shoulder, all the way up to her cheek. Then he said softly, "Tell me what the doctors said? Did they get the bullet out? Is the baby okay?"

Sandy smiled. "The doctor said we were very lucky. The baby's fine." A delicious warmth spread through her when Tristan gently pressed his forehead against hers. She closed her eyes as he pulled away just enough to kiss her.

But behind her lids, new images appeared, of bullets flying and blood spattering. She frowned at him.

"What about you?" she asked, looking him over. He was dressed in scrubs. His face was scratched, probably by branches, and his eyes were sunken with fatigue, but he was here. He was alive.

He nodded. His hand tightened on hers. "I'm fine."

"Are you really okay? And what about Boudreau?"

"He's here. We're in Houma. Terrebonne Parish Hospital. They're releasing Boudreau this afternoon. One of the rifle bullets parted his hair, on the wrong side, no less," he said, the frown fading a little as the corner of his mouth turned up. "They admitted him because the slug that hit him in the forearm kind of pulverized the bone."

"Oh, no," Sandy said. "He won't be able to get along with one arm."

"Okay, *pulverized* is probably the wrong word. They put several pins in it and they think it's going to heal okay. It'll hurt him when it rains, though."

"I hope it does. Heal, not hurt."

"He's been asking about you. He wants to come see you as soon as it's okay with the doctors."

"Really? I'd have thought he'd be chomping at the bit to get back home."

"Well, that, too."

She paused to look at him. The light in the room was getting brighter as the sun rose outside. "Tristan, please tell me. You're really okay? Have you been here the whole time?"

He shook his head. "I had to be debriefed. They flew me to DC. I guess they wanted to see for themselves that I was alive."

She frowned at him. "Really?"

He gave her a crooked smile. "Just kidding. It's standard procedure to be transported in for a debriefing after a…situation."

"You look exhausted," Sandy said. "How are you? Have you been able to rest? Did the doctors look at your leg?"

He angled his head. "I'm fine, really."

"Fine? That's all you have to say after everything that's happened?"

Tristan lowered the guardrail and leaned forward. He rested his palm on top of her head and stroked her forehead with his thumb.

"Homeland Security had me thoroughly checked out, mentally and physically. I must have talked with every acronym in the city. FBI, CIA, NSA. But they also sent me to Walter Reed for a complete physical. I might have to have surgery, but it can wait awhile."

"Surgery. On your leg? Oh, Tristan, maybe they can fix it," she said, squeezing his hand.

He frowned. "We'll see. Anyhow, I've been back here since yesterday evening. Spent about three hours talking with the sheriff, then I came to see you about eight-thirty, but you were asleep. They let me stay in here, a booby prize, I guess, since they wouldn't tell me anything specific except that you and the baby were resting comfortably." He stood and bent over to kiss her on the lips.

For a moment, Sandy floated in the blissful knowledge that Tristan was real, he was alive and nothing could change that.

When she opened her eyes and took her first good look at him, she saw that his face was drawn and pale. He looked worried and—as she'd told him—exhausted. More than anything in the world, she wanted him to kiss her again. She wanted to feel the vibrancy of his skin, the warmth of his lips. She wanted to soak in everything about him that proved to her that he was alive and real and here.

But because of the way he looked, all she said was, "They got them, didn't they? The bad guys?"

The frown returned to Tristan's face. "Oh, you surely remember that. Lee had told Echols, the guy on dry land, that he was sending a helicopter to strafe the whole area and kill us and them. That's the reason he finally decided to call the sheriff for me.

"The sheriff managed to get the Coast Guard to send two helicopters to intercept Lee's bird and send it running back to where it came from. Then one copter airlifted you and Boudreau here, and the other one picked up our two friends and me."

"I remember floating really high up but I thought that was a dream."

"Nope. No dream."

Sandy stared at him, openmouthed. *Butterfly wings.* "Not butterfly wings, helicopter propellers," she muttered.

"What?"

"Nothing. And they put you and those two killers in one basket? Tristan. They could have killed you."

He shook his head. "They were too happy not to be killed by Lee. I understand they're in DC now, singing their little hearts out to Homeland Security and the FBI about Vernon Lee and his plot to bring down the US from the inside by supplying automatic handguns to kids on the street and organized crime."

"Have they caught Lee?"

Tristan shook his head. "They can't find him. I was told there was evidence that he'd been shot, or had shot himself. But all that was found in his penthouse office in the Lee Building in San Francisco was a gun with his fingerprints on it and a fair amount of his blood. I don't think anybody connected with this case is going to make an assumption about whether he's dead. Not after they all assumed that I was."

"So he could still be out there?"

Tristan didn't answer for a beat. "He could be," he finally said.

"You don't think he is? Do you think he's dead?" she asked on a yawn.

Tristan frowned and was silent for a long time. "I don't. I think I'd have to say show me the body."

"Tristan," she said. "I have to tell you something. Lee Drilling sent a really nice condolence letter and they have set up a trust fund for the little bean."

"A trust fund? Screw that."

Sandy shivered. "I know. It kind of makes me nauseated to think about it." She lay quietly for a moment. "I might be sleepy," she murmured.

Tristan smiled at her. "You'd better sleep while you can. Everybody from the sheriff to the media to the government's going to want to talk to you, too, now that you're awake."

"I've already talked to them," she protested.

"Apparently not enough. I was given the times by my boss at Homeland Security and told that the alphabet agencies would like me to be at the interrogation, too."

He brought her fingers to his lips and kissed them. "I'm afraid all this will go on for a long time. I'm sorry." He sat there, pressing her hand to his cheek, that frown back on his face.

"What's wrong?" she asked.

He shook his head. "Nothing."

She pulled her hand away and took a long breath to try to push through the drowsiness. "Oh, no. No," she said sternly. "You are not going to keep on doing that. I won't stand for it."

Tristan lifted his gaze to his wife's eyes, which were blazing. But he couldn't hold it. Anger and fear shone from their depths. He stood and walked over to the window, where the sun was just coming up.

What could he do, if anything, to repair their broken hearts? They'd grown so far apart during the past few years. And then all this had happened and he'd let her down so completely that he was sure she could never forgive him.

He'd done it for her and their baby, and to try to stop a murderous terrorist, but had he lost everything important to him in the process? "Sandy," he said without turning around. "I'm sorry."

"What?"

He turned awkwardly, favoring his bad leg. "I let you down in so many ways. I hope you can forgive me."

"For-forgive you?" she stammered. "Are you kidding me?"

He closed his eyes, pain wrenching his sore heart. "I know. It's not enough, but I swear to you, I'll do everything I can to make it up to you if you'll let me."

"Tristan, there's only one thing I want you to do."

He nodded. "Of course. Anything."

"Come here and turn on the overhead light."

Baffled, he did as she said. When he looked at her, her face was glowing as it had when she'd first found out she was pregnant. He almost gasped aloud. From the time they were nine years old, he'd always thought she was the prettiest thing he'd ever seen. She still was.

"Unless I dreamed it, too, there should be a big manila folder around here somewhere. Do you see it? I'm pretty sure the doctor left it here." She looked around.

He saw it lying near the sink. He picked it up. "Is this it?"

"Yes. It's my sonogram. They printed it out so I could show you. They made a DVD for us, too."

"Of what?" he asked, still confused about what she was doing and saying.

When he looked at her, her eyes were wet with tears. Fear clawed at his insides. "Sandy? You said everything was fine. Is something wrong with the baby?"

"Just look at it." Her voice was tight with emotion.

He took out the glossy photograph and looked at it, his hand shaking with the force of his pounding pulse. "This is the bean?" he asked, angling his head one way and then the other. "Sandy, what is it? What am I looking at?"

A sniffle made him glance at her. "Are you crying? God, Sandy. Just tell me. What's wrong with him?"

"Can you see him?" She traced a shape on the photo with her finger. "His head, his back, his little legs?"

Tristan did. He traced the tiny head, the curve of the little back. The perfect arms and legs. "Oh," he said. "He looks perfect. Please tell me he's okay." His voice broke and his eyes stung. "Please."

Sandy didn't say anything. She just kept her gaze on the sonogram. Tristan turned back to study it. Then he noticed something odd. He frowned. "What's that?" he asked, pointing.

"Hmm?" Sandy murmured innocently.

"That." He pointed to a small opaque object that appeared to be clutched by the bean's impossibly tiny hand. "It looks like—" He stopped. He bent to look closer.

"Like what, Tris?" she whispered.

"It looks like a—" He shook his head. If he thought his pulse was pounding before, now it was slamming against his breastbone like a battering ram. "But that's impossible," he muttered.

Sandy chuckled softly. "You'd think so, but there it is."

"How— What—"

"I don't know how, but that is the bullet that shot me."

"But that's his little hand. He's *holding* it." Tristan looked up. "What—what do the doctors say?"

"They can't explain it. They say that it should have still been going fast enough to go right through me. They said they'd have expected it to do a lot of damage to—" she swallowed and gestured vaguely "—you know."

"I don't understand," Tristan said as much to give his brain time to catch up with what she was telling him as because it was the truth. How had a lethal bullet penetrated Sandy's skin and come to rest in their unborn baby's hand? "It looks like he caught it—"

"—to stop it from ripping through my kidney. A few people are calling it a miracle."

He shook his head in wonder. "It looks miraculous to me."

Sandy smiled at him through her tears. "That would be a total of two."

"Two?"

"Two miracles," she said, pushing up into a sitting position and reaching for him. "The first one was you coming back to me."

Tristan sat down on the edge of the bed and pulled her into his arms and kissed her, gently, then more deeply, until when they finally stopped, both of them were breathless.

"Hmm. Actually," Tristan murmured, "I'd have to say it makes for three miracles."

"Three?" Sandy stared at him. "What's the third one?"

Tristan pressed a sweet kiss to her temple. "That the three of us are here together. I love you, San. With all my stubborn, stubborn heart. And that's no lying lie."

Sandy laughed through her tears and kissed her husband. Her heart soared and the little bean kicked.

Epilogue

Several weeks later

"But you promised to bring your wedding dress," Sandy said to Maddy. She was sitting in an overstuffed chair in the cramped living room of the mobile home Tristan had gotten set up on the site of his family home that had burned. When the windows were open, there was still a charcoal smell in the air. "I wanted to see you in it since I couldn't go to the wedding."

"Honey," Maddy said, "that dress would have taken its own oversize suitcase. It would have cost a fortune to bring it and I didn't want to drag it around on our honeymoon."

"Okay, fine. But I want to see all your photos. We'll tell Tristan to put them up on the TV screen."

Maddy sat down in a kitchen chair and looked assessingly at Sandy. "You look good. Are you really doing okay?"

"You mean except for being confined to bed for my entire pregnancy? Sure. I'm fine."

Maddy picked up the sonogram photo off the table and looked at it again. "This is unbelievable. So they don't want you moving around too much because he might let go of the bullet?"

"Yes. Apparently it could be dangerous, and they don't want to have to go into the uterus prior to his birth."

"Well, your sonogram went viral. Your baby is famous before he's even born."

"I know. That's disgusting. If I can help it, he'll never know."

"You're not going to tell him?"

"Well, not until he's twenty-five or so."

Maddy smiled at her. "Sandy, I'm so glad nobody was hurt any worse than they were. What an ordeal you had."

"No more than you being kidnapped and Zach being shot."

"Oh, honey, if I'd had to go through losing Zach like you had to live through losing Tristan, I'd have died."

Sandy rubbed her very large tummy. "I might have, if not for the bean here."

"You're so brave," Maddy said.

"No. It's Tristan who's brave."

Maddy glanced toward the door. "He looks pretty good."

"He's doing better. He almost ruined the muscle tissue he has left on that right calf, with all the running we had to do. And he still hasn't gained back his weight. He's had to spend hours every week in hearings, interrogations and interviews, but they have finally proven that the voice on the recordings is Vernon Lee's."

"Right. I see summaries of what's going on, since I was involved in the case at the beginning."

"It's eating Tristan up, though, that there's no proof that Lee is actually dead. I don't know if he can rest until he can view the man's body."

Maddy shook her head. "The prevailing opinion is that he's alive. There was a lot of blood, but there have been cases in the past where people have bled themselves and saved up their blood so they could be declared dead by exsanguination."

"Ugh. Where are Zach and Tristan? I'm hungry."

"I know, right? How long does it take to grill some burgers."

"And bacon!"

Maddy laughed. "You've done a 180 on bacon, I see. Even the word made you nauseous when you were first pregnant."

At that moment, Tristan and Zach came in, laughing. Sandy noticed that Tristan was not limping as much as he sometimes did. And he looked happy. He and Zach had been best friends practically all their lives. Male friendships were odd and interesting. The two of them were acting as though they saw each other every day.

"If you'd been there, Boudreau and I would have had to carry you kicking and screaming across that bridge," Tristan said, laughing.

Zach scowled as he set a plate of grilled burgers on the kitchen counter. "I'm not that afraid of heights. You have to get me a little above sea level before I start panicking."

"Lunch is served," Tristan said, walking over and bending to plant a kiss on top of Sandy's head.

"Oh, Tris, come on. No buns? No mayonnaise? No cheese? And where's my bacon?"

Zach was already headed toward the refrigerator. He pulled out a tray that contained everything, even the bacon. "Right here."

Zach and Tristan fought over the biggest burger while

Sandy and Maddy sat and watched them act like six-year-olds.

"Zach," Maddy said. "You two are like bulls in a china shop. You're going to break the whole kitchen if you keep scuffling." Finally she got up and forced her way between them.

"My turn," she said.

Tristan emerged victorious, with the giant burger captured in a bun. He squirted mayonnaise on it and added cheese and bacon and brought it over to Sandy.

"Here you go, Ms. I'm-Eating-for-Two." He handed her the plate, then sat on the arm of her chair with his hand on her tummy.

"I can't eat all that," she protested as she prepared to take a huge bite.

She looked up at him and caught him watching Maddy and Zach.

"You've missed Zach, haven't you?"

Typical for him, he didn't answer.

"You might get to see him more if you take that position in DC." She felt him stiffen, but she went on. "I'd be perfectly happy there. Anywhere, actually, as long as I've got you there with me."

He looked down at her, his expression soft with a mixture of sadness and humor. "You like me," he said teasingly.

"I cannot deny that I do," she responded.

"What if I didn't go to DC?" he said, looking back at Maddy and Zach. "Those two were born to be government agents. Look at them. They're totally in sync. I was never good at it."

"No. You have an honest face and an honest and romantic heart."

"I was going to say I didn't like it. Anyhow, I happened to overhear a conversation and I almost got killed for it. I'm not interested in a steady diet of danger."

Sandy took a deep breath as a profound relief settled on her, dissolving the heavy cloud of worry she'd been carrying around for months. Carefully she said, "What are you thinking you might want to do?"

"I've talked to a guy who's a large-animal veterinarian in Houma. He could use an assistant a few days a week. I think I'll try that. The rest of the time I plan to start working on a house."

She couldn't stop the grin that spread on her face or the love that swelled in her heart. "You're going to build it here, where your home was?"

Tristan nodded. "Is that all right with you?"

Sandy smiled as the bean kicked the side of her growing baby bump. She took a bite of her huge burger without answering him.

Everything was all right with her world, because Tristan DuChaud loved her.

* * * * *

COMING NEXT MONTH FROM

HARLEQUIN®

INTRIGUE

Available June 16, 2015

#1575 SURRENDERING TO THE SHERIFF
Sweetwater Ranch • by Delores Fossen

Discovering Kendall O'Neal being held at gunpoint at his ranch isn't the homecoming sheriff Aiden Braddock expects. Kendall's captors are demanding he destroy evidence in exchange for the Texas attorney's life... and the life of their unborn baby.

#1576 UNDER FIRE
Brothers in Arms: Retribution • by Carol Ericson

Agent Max Duvall needs Dr. Ava Whitman's help to break free from the brainwashing that Tempest—the covert ops agency they work for—has subjected him to...but he's going to have to keep the agency from killing her first.

#1577 SHELTERED
Corcoran Team: Bulletproof Bachelors • by HelenKay Dimon

Undercover agent Holt Kingston has one mission: to infiltrate a dangerous cult. But when the compound's ruthless leader has a gorgeous former member in his sights, single-minded Holt won't rest until Lindsey Pike is safe.

#1578 LAWMAN PROTECTION
The Ranger Brigade • by Cindi Myers

A killer is lurking in Colorado, and reporter Emma Wade is sniffing around Captain Graham Ellison's crime scene. As much as he doesn't want a civilian accessing his case, Graham will need to keep Emma close if he is going to keep her alive.

#1579 LEVERAGE
Omega Sector • by Janie Crouch

Reclusive pilot Dylan Branson's mission to escort Shelby Keelan to Omega Sector goes awry after his plane is sabotaged midair. With both their lives in danger, Dylan no longer thinks Shelby is just a job—or that he can let her go once it's over.

#1580 THE DETECTIVE • by Adrienne Giordano

Passion ignites when interior designer Lexi Vanderbilt teams up with hardened homicide detective Brodey Hayward to solve a cold case murder. But will Lexi's ambition make them both targets of a killer?

———

YOU CAN FIND MORE INFORMATION ON UPCOMING HARLEQUIN® TITLES, FREE EXCERPTS AND MORE AT WWW.HARLEQUIN.COM.

HICNM0615

REQUEST YOUR FREE BOOKS!
2 FREE NOVELS PLUS 2 FREE GIFTS!

H HARLEQUIN®

INTRIGUE

BREATHTAKING ROMANTIC SUSPENSE

YES! Please send me 2 FREE Harlequin® Intrigue novels and my 2 FREE gifts (gifts are worth about $10). After receiving them, if I don't wish to receive any more books, I can return the shipping statement marked "cancel." If I don't cancel, I will receive 6 brand-new novels every month and be billed just $4.74 per book in the U.S. or $5.49 per book in Canada. That's a savings of at least 12% off the cover price! It's quite a bargain! Shipping and handling is just 50¢ per book in the U.S. and 75¢ per book in Canada.* I understand that accepting the 2 free books and gifts places me under no obligation to buy anything. I can always return a shipment and cancel at any time. Even if I never buy another book, the two free books and gifts are mine to keep forever.

182/382 HDN GH3D

Name _____ (PLEASE PRINT)

Address _____ Apt. #

City _____ State/Prov. _____ Zip/Postal Code

Signature (if under 18, a parent or guardian must sign)

Mail to the **Reader Service**:
IN U.S.A.: P.O. Box 1867, Buffalo, NY 14240-1867
IN CANADA: P.O. Box 609, Fort Erie, Ontario L2A 5X3

**Are you a subscriber to Harlequin® Intrigue books
and want to receive the larger-print edition?
Call 1-800-873-8635 or visit www.ReaderService.com.**

* Terms and prices subject to change without notice. Prices do not include applicable taxes. Sales tax applicable in N.Y. Canadian residents will be charged applicable taxes. Offer not valid in Quebec. This offer is limited to one order per household. Not valid for current subscribers to Harlequin Intrigue books. All orders subject to credit approval. Credit or debit balances in a customer's account(s) may be offset by any other outstanding balance owed by or to the customer. Please allow 4 to 6 weeks for delivery. Offer available while quantities last.

Your Privacy—The Reader Service is committed to protecting your privacy. Our Privacy Policy is available online at www.ReaderService.com or upon request from the Reader Service.

We make a portion of our mailing list available to reputable third parties that offer products we believe may interest you. If you prefer that we not exchange your name with third parties, or if you wish to clarify or modify your communication preferences, please visit us at www.ReaderService.com/consumerschoice or write to us at Reader Service Preference Service, P.O. Box 9062, Buffalo, NY 14240-9062. Include your complete name and address.

HII5

SPECIAL EXCERPT FROM

HARLEQUIN

INTRIGUE

*Navy SEAL "Rip" Cord Schafer's mission is not a
one-man operation, but never in his wildest dreams did
he imagine teaming up with a woman: Covert Cowboy
operative Tracie Kosart.*

Read on for a sneak peek at
NAVY SEAL NEWLYWED,
the newest installment from
Elle James's
COVERT COWBOYS, INC.

"How do I know you really work for Hank?"

"You don't. But has anyone else shown up and told
you he's your contact?" She raised her eyebrows, the
saucy expression doing funny things to his insides. "So,
do you trust me, or not?"

His lips curled upward on the ends. "I'll go with not."

"Oh, come on, sweetheart." She batted her pretty green
eyes and gave him a sexy smile. "What's not to trust?"

His gaze scraped over her form. "I expected a cowboy,
not a…"

"Cow*girl*?" Her smile sank and she slipped into the
driver's seat. Her lips firmed into a straight line. "Are
you coming or not? If you're dead set on a cowboy, I'll
contact Hank and tell him to send a male replacement.
But then he'd have to come up with another plan."

"I'm interested in how you and Hank plan to help.
Frankly, I'd rather my SEAL team had my six."

"Yeah, but you're deceased. Using your SEAL team would only alert your assassin that you aren't as dead as the navy claims you are. How long do you think you'll last once that bit of news leaks out?"

His lips pressed together. "I'd survive."

"By going undercover? Then you still won't have the backing of your team, and we're back to the original plan." She grinned. "Me."

Rip sighed. "Fine. I want to head back to Honduras and trace the weapons back to where they're coming from. What's Hank's plan?"

"For me to work with you." She pulled a large envelope from between her seat and the console and handed it across to him. "Everything we need is in that packet."

Rip riffled through the contents of the packet, glancing at a passport with his picture on it as well as a name he'd never seen. "Chuck Gideon?"

"Better get used to it."

"Speaking of names…we've already kissed and you haven't told me who you are." Rip glanced her way briefly. "Is it a secret? Do you have a shady past or are you related to someone important?"

"For this mission, I'm related to someone important." She twisted her lips and sent a crooked grin his way. "You. For the purpose of this operation, you can call me Phyllis. Phyllis Gideon. I'll be your wife."

Don't miss
NAVY SEAL NEWLYWED,
available June 2015 wherever
Harlequin® Intrigue® books and ebooks are sold

www.Harlequin.com

Copyright © 2015 by Mary Jernigan

HIEXP0615

3 1491 01174 2388

THE WORLD IS BETTER
WITH

Romance

Harlequin has everything from contemporary, passionate and heartwarming to suspenseful and inspirational stories.

Whatever your mood,
we have a romance just for you!

Connect with us to find your next great read, special offers and more.

/HarlequinBooks

@HarlequinBooks

www.HarlequinBlog.com

www.Harlequin.com/Newsletters

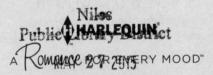

HARLEQUIN®

A *Romance* FOR EVERY MOOD™

Niles
Public Library District

MAY 2 7 2015

Niles, Illinois 60714

www.Harlequin.com

SERIESHALOAD2015